Dream Ink Publications Presents

I0552583

Love, Lies 'N Betrayal 2

"Be careful with your actions, 'cause karma is a BITCH!"

By: Courtney Simone

Love, Lies 'N Betrayal 2

Copyright © 2019 by Courtney Simmons

Published by Dream Ink Publications

ISBN 978-1-7338530-1-9

"*Karma* - payback for the actions taken upon someone with or without intentions of hurting them."

- Courtney Simone

Table of Contents

Chapter 1

"Confirmation"

At the baby shower, I couldn't believe my eyes. Just when I thought Michelle had come to her senses, realizing that she wasn't wanted there, she showed up. No way in hell could I believe what I saw, and I really didn't want to, but it was true. Michelle and Norris were fucking around with each other. Funny thing was, Norris and I were just starting to rebuild our friendship and learning to co-parent.

We were cool with each other, we weren't bickering anymore, and I was coming around, after all that he'd done to me. I didn't want to be a bitter baby mama, causing problems in his life, but it was obvious he wasn't thinking the same way I was. I didn't understand it. Why didn't he mention to me that he was messing around with my sister? I thought we were cool enough with each other now.

I should have known. How did I not see this coming? She was desperate for love and she'd been hating on us since back in the day. *She probably wanted him since then*, I thought to myself.

And Norris, the player, manipulator and liar. This guy's entire life was a mystery. He lived in secrets and couldn't tell the truth to save his life. I let myself down for believing that he'd changed. For being naive to the lies I was told, and the fake love shown to me. My stupid-ass!

My own flesh and blood did me dirty and turned her back. That hurt me deeper than what Chanel did. The one that hated Norris the most when we dated... The one who tried convincing me multiple times to leave him because he was no good for me... only for her to ease in where she didn't belong. Yeah, that chick!

She may have not known that he was my kid's father, but she knew the special place he held in my heart and what he once meant to me. Out of all the guys in the world, why him? I couldn't help but wonder if Chanel was behind this or if my sister parted ways with me to make a move on him.

These days, Chanel was just as miserable as Michelle; I wouldn't doubt it. Now, here I was, beefing with two women that once meant everything to me - my best friend and my sister. People who I once enjoyed being around, I now hated to be in their presence. Both of them now had ties to someone I did, for the rest of my life. I didn't know what that meant for Norris and I at that point. How would it work? Would they interfere? But no matter how I felt about these situations, I had a kid to think about and hard decisions to make.

I was dying to know how they ended up messing around and how long it'd been going on. Did he initiate their relationship or was it his petty-ass sister who put the two together? When did they even start talking? I hoped they weren't together the past few months. Norris and I just fucked a few months ago at his place. It was disgusting to even think about. It unsettled me, knowing that we fucked the same dude, because I wasn't that type of chick. I wouldn't fuck with a dude knowing one of my girls dealt with him; but clearly, that meant nothing to her.

I thought Norris was coming around. Growing into a smart, responsible man. Instead, he was still a cold-hearted, dirty dog. Despite how upsetting the situation made me, I called Norris. I was calm, with no intentions of arguing. I just wanted answers.

"Hey, Norris."

"Yeah, what's up, Tara," he responded. He knew I would be calling, once I saw what he did at Josh and Gracie's shower. So, I got straight to the point.

"I saw you and Michelle hugged up. Didn't know y'all were messing around. What was that about?"

"Yeah, we mess around from time to time, but I wouldn't call it a relationship; fuck friends, if you want to be technical. We party together, fuck and chill sometimes. That's about it."

"So, you didn't see any wrong in messing with my damn sister?" I went on to ask, as my voice got louder.

"It's not that serious, Tara! Why you arguing with me? I wasn't in this by myself," Norris replied.

"Oh, don't worry, she's gonna get checked too."

Why are you worrying about who I'm fuckin', you don't want me anymore, right? Shit, for all I know, you could be fucking one of my guys, but I ain't trippin'!"

"You know damn well I don't want your ass. Don't take that little fuck session we had at your place serious because it wasn't. I fucked you with no feelings involved. And, you're right, maybe I should chill because who you fuck ain't none of my business. It works both ways. So, if I'm fuckin' one of your homeboys, don't worry about it."

"So, you're saying that you are fuckin' one of my niggas? Well, which one is it?" Norris asked, uneasily.

"Who I'm fuckin' ain't got shit to do with you, like you told me. Just know, whoever I'm sexing, I'm doing him better than I did you," I said, right before I hung up.

I sat on my bed, my eyes full of tears, but for some reason I couldn't drop them. My head started thumping in pain. As I sat there in bed, I held my head, thinking about all the shit I went through. I wondered what else I would have to deal with, when it came to the same people I was done with but couldn't seem to escape.

Norris never called or texted back after I hung up. Not once did he apologize or try to see how he could ease my mind and lift the pain, but that was Norris. Same ol' Norris I dealt with years ago. Selfish Norris that only gave a fuck about himself! I was used to it; it wasn't nothing new. I wasn't going to let them get the best of me, though. I was happy with Daddy and only focusing on us.

When I woke up the next day, I saw a letter on the kitchen counter that read, "Good morning, baby! Hope you rested well last night. Sorry I'm not there for you to wake up to. I had to get to the office early. I will call you when I get some time. See you soon! Anthony."

I smiled from ear to ear. He made me forget all that happened with Norris and everyone else. Daddy was the real deal. They say, 'Third time's a charm,' and I was starting to believe it. Someway, somehow, he always turned my frown upside down and turned a bad day into a good one. I was starting to put my all into him. I even let my guard down, a little bit more at a time, and I was allowing him to treat me how I deserved to be treated.

I was still scared of getting hurt again, but I was trying to think positively about us. I started to become less doubtful about him leaving or hurting me. He'd shown me that he was different from the rest. That he appreciates and loves me. Going out of his way to please me and make me happy. Most of all, he never allows me to degrade myself and helps me understand my worth. He is everything any woman would die for; even me, if I had to die behind him.

After getting dressed, I left the house, and about five minutes later, my phone rung. It was an unknown number. I hardly ever answered unknown numbers. Almost every time, it was either somebody I didn't want to talk to or a damn joke. I wasn't in the mood for either, but for some reason I answered this time. Guess who it was... Norris!

I wanted to hang up, but I also wanted to know what he could possibly have to say to me. Before taking the DNA test and finding out he was actually Mani's father, ignoring him was easy. Now, not so much. He could be contacting me to check on his kid. The last thing I wanted to do was keep a loving father away from his child. Now, it was like I was obligated to speak to him, even if I wasn't thrilled to.

He started off by apologizing. He apologized to me for the choices he made and told me he knew it wasn't right. He told me how much he still loved me and how happy finding out he was a father made him. He talked about how he never wanted to hurt me and that it wasn't his intention. I heard him out, although I thought it was all bullshit. It sounded good, but I kept how manipulative he was in the back of my mind.

I didn't say a word. I let him say everything he needed to. Then, he asked me if I could come by his house later to talk about how things were going to be. I wasn't sure about that. It didn't sit right with me that he wanted me to come over to talk about something that could be discussed over the phone. He could have said what he needed to, while we were on the phone at that time. I told him I would think about it and let him know. Something was definitely fishy about the situation.

I didn't want to go over to his place alone, but I couldn't take Daddy with me either.

That would be very disrespectful, I thought.

They'd never met or been around each other and I didn't have anyone else to go with me. I called Gracie to get her thoughts about all of this. I knew if there was anyone that would be honest with me, no matter what, it would be her. It wasn't like I had anyone else to turn to anyway.

"Hey, girl! Are you busy?"

"No, I'm just up watching my shows. What's going on, boo?"

"So, I need your honest opinion and advice on something."

"I've always been honest and forever will be. Talk to me!"

"Ok, so… it's true. Norris and Michelle are fuckin' around with each other. Our eyes were not playing tricks on us. Well, anyway, Norris and I got into a disagreement on the phone about it. After arguing with him, I hung up and didn't speak to him. He called me the next day and apologized about everything, explaining how he loved me and never wanted to hurt me. He poured his heart out to me. Blah, blah, blah! Ok, cool. But the strange part about it was that he invited me over and said he wanted to talk. I don't understand why I need to go to his place when we can talk about whatever it is he wants to talk about on the phone. It's not sitting right with me. If I go, I would have to go alone because I don't have anyone else to go with. Anthony can't go, and I know you ain't going. What do you think about this situation? Why do you think he wants me to come over?"

"Well, Tara, let me just start off by saying that you are right, I'm not going. I just don't feel like all that drama. It is a bit strange, though. What I think you should do is just ask him! Ask him why he wants you to come over. See what he says. Maybe it's a good reason behind all of it. Communication is everything; especially, when a child is involved. If you are done with him, like you say you are, then go. But if he doesn't want you to come over about y'all's kid, like he said, then don't go. But you won't know anything until you ask," Gracie suggested, before ending the call.

Maybe it was a good reason behind it. I hesitated on asking Norris, though. He hardly ever told the truth. If he had tricks up his sleeve, he definitely wasn't going to tell me about it. Hell, he kept shit from me I was obligated to know. After talking all my shit and contemplating not calling, I ended up calling him.

"Norris?"

"Yo! Wassup?

"We spoke the other day about meeting up and I wanted to know if it was something we could talk about on the phone or was there a particular reason you wanted me to come by."

"I wanted you to bring baby girl with you, so her and I could bond while we talked. Something wrong? If you're not up for it, it's cool."

"As long as it will only be the three of us there, I'm fine with it!"

"Come by tomorrow. I'll be home around 3pm. Will that work for you?"

"It's perfect, actually. See you tomorrow."

"Ok, be easy."

The call turned out better than I thought it would. My baby deserves her father in her life... Now that we knew who it really was. As long as we had no interference in our confrontation, it would be all good. Co-parenting with Norris may not be so bad after all.

Chapter 2

"Baby Daddy Drama"

When baby girl and I pulled up, I still felt anxious about being there. It wasn't like any of the other times I went over. I sat in the car for a while, before heading to his door. I observed my surroundings and looked for whatever I could find that showed something wasn't right. The first sign I got - besides my gut - that something didn't sit right with me, I was leaving and I wasn't going to turn back.

After sitting in the car for some time, I decided to go in and see how it would go. I got baby girl out the car seat, walked up the stairs and knocked on the door. While I waited for Norris to answer, I heard a lot of noise. It sounded like a female's laugh.

I was standing in the hallway of an apartment complex, so it could have come from anywhere. I wasn't 100% sure it was coming from his apartment. I started thinking, *maybe I'm just paranoid and trippin'*, so I didn't think anything else of it. That was until he opened the door.

I walked in with baby girl in my arms, looked to the left and Chanel was there, sitting on the couch, with Michelle sitting right next to her. They were just as surprised to see me walk through the door as I was to see them sitting on the damn couch. I had my daughter with me, I wasn't warned nor prepared to deal with them. Now, I was pissed at Norris for keeping me in the dark and not telling me they would be there. The worst part about it was that he used my daughter and put her in the middle of all of this.

Things were still heated between Chanel and I. I wasn't feelin' Michelle either. With Michelle and I, things were just getting hotter, because there were some things we still hadn't addressed. I was still pissed about her and Norris fucking around. He had some nerve bringing us all together, after he knew how I felt about them both. How could he think this was ok? What the fuck was really wrong with Norris? He started to make me think that maybe he was snorting the coke he was selling.

When I parked outside and walked up the steps, although I didn't feel right about all of it, I still came; but walking into this damn intervention made me wish I had followed my gut. Had I not ignored my woman's intuition, neither me or my daughter would have been standing there.

Apparently, Norris planned what seemed to be a secret mediation for us to hash out what it was we hated each other over and squash our beef. Being that we all were in his life and at one point were so close, he thought it was important. I thought it was too, until I got to this point in my life. I no longer gave a fuck about rekindling friendships that included betrayal, broken promises and lies.

It was too late for all of that. In fact, I couldn't see any of us being friendly with one another or seeing eye to eye again. I had unfinished business with these two women that I needed to take care of on my own. Norris was on my bad side as well, but unfortunately, he was important to someone that was very important to me. Cutting him off like I did before was almost impossible.

I stood next to the door with my daughter in my arms and my back against the wall, posted up. I was waiting and ready for whatever these bitches wanted to do. I had been wanting to throw hands with these bitches for a long time. So, if one moved funny or made me feel uncomfortable, I was popping them in the face.

Norris started talking about why he brought us all together. The look on their faces when he said that Armani was his kid explained a lot. Clearly, they hadn't heard about the DNA test and the truth.

"Damn THOT!" I heard one of them whisper, right before they both started laughing.

I ignored the comment that was made because they had some nerve after what they'd done. Shortly after, they both started talking about why they were upset with me.

Yeah, yeah, yeah! I said to myself. The shit they said went in one ear and out the other. You know why? Because I tried reaching out to both of them, in the beginning, when I first saw that things were going left with us. They gave me the cold shoulder, while sticking their asses out for me to kiss.

The shit they did to me would take time for me to heal from. Ain't like I was hoping or rushing for it to happen anyway. So, guess what? I let them talk, ignoring every word they said. When they were done, I stated facts about the entire situation. I got deep and said things they obviously weren't ready to hear, because after that, they were ready to throw blows.

Chanel got up off the couch, cursing and pointing her fingers, while Norris held her back. I sat my daughter on another chair, at a distance, making sure I didn't put her in harm's way. I was waiting for Chanel to come at me, so I could do the things to her I should have done a long time ago. I kept talking, and while I went towards Chanel, Michelle jumped up.

"So, you're ready to fight your own sister to protect this bitch?"

"Unlike you, she held me down!" Michelle replied.

"Held you down? This bitch ain't did shit for you but make you a pathetic bitch just like her!"

"Pathetic? So, I'm pathetic 'cause I took your man? Let me remind you, your husband loves this pathetic bitch. Enough to leave your tiresome-ass alone," Chanel yelled.

"You're a cheap ho, that's why! You couldn't find a man to love you, so you went after mine because you wanted the life I have. He will never love or treat you like he did me! Remember that!" I hollered at Chanel.

"Y'all, chill out!" Norris hollered at all of us.

"Let them bitches go, Norris. Let they ass loose! I'm ready to beat these bitches. Let them go," I told him.

"Man, take my baby and leave. This has gotten way out of hand," Norris yelled.

"No! I'm not leaving until I fight," I hollered back.

Baby girl was crying in the background. I was so caught up in the moment that I didn't know how long she'd been hollering. I was unable to hear her cries over the hollering and bickering I did with peasants who were beneath me.

As Michelle and Chanel continued to mouth off, I grabbed my daughter.

"This ain't over!" I told them.

"Take your baldheaded-ass daughter and leave, bitch," Michelle hollered.

As bad as I wanted to turn around and pop her in the mouth, my daughter and I headed out the door, down the stairs and to the car, still in shock about what just happened. Nothing was established from that mediation, except built-up anger and hate. In fact, it was now worse than what it was before I came.

When we got home, I was overdue for a good meal and some extraordinary sex. My day was rough. I knew Daddy would take care of me, though, like no other; he always has! When I walked in the door, I started to believe he was a mind reader.

Immediately, as I stepped foot in the place, a pleasant scent of well-seasoned steak and vegetables filled the room. My plate was being made, as I walked in the door. As soon as he handed my plate over to me, I began to stuff my face with steak, broccoli, asparagus, onions, bell peppers and mashed potatoes.

He grabbed baby girl out of my arms and fed her, before running my bubble bath. When I came home, I didn't have to do anything. He had my lingerie laid out already. He even gave baby girl a bath, after feeding her, and then put her to bed. I loved everything about him. If I had continued to brush him off and not give him the opportunity to enter my world, I knew I would have regretted it.

After I got out the bathtub, Daddy was sitting on the edge of the bed naked, waiting for me with lotion in his hand. He moisturized my body, as he gave me a full-body massage. He applied just enough pressure to release the tension, as his nice, warm hands ran across my caramel skin. My eyes closed, slowly, as his soft fingers caressed my body, relaxing me.

He stood up at the edge of the bed and dragged me towards him, leaving my feet to hang off. He started grinding up on my ass, as he continued to rub me down. Daddy gripped my waist and pulled my ass back towards him, with force, imitating what he did when he sexed me. Hearing the clapping of my ass hitting his body turned me on. I lifted my ass up higher, putting a deep arch in my back, hoping that he would be able to slide deeply in me the next time he pulled me back. Just as I hoped, it happened.

"Uh yeah, yeah! Yeah, Daddy," I moaned.

"Come on, baby! Throw that ass back! Yeah, just like that! Ride Daddy like you missed him," Daddy hollered, while slapping me on my ass almost every time I threw it back.

I loved when he talked dirty to me, just as much as he enjoyed when I did it to him. Even though, when he beat it up, it made it hard for me to talk.

"Come…come on, Daddy! Ke…keep going! Put it all in me! I'm about to cum! I'm about to cum all over this good dick."

"Me too, baby! I'm about to nut in this warm pussy!"

I hollered, loudly. I shuffled around the bed, gripping the sheets tightly. He pulled me closer and closer, going deeper and faster!"

"Uhhhh!" I hollered.

"Ouuuu!" He moaned.

We both came at the same time. He kissed me on my cheek and said, "Girl, I can't live without y'all," while gripping and squeezing my pussy all in one hand.

With a hectic-ass day from all the baby daddy drama, a nice massage and good sex was exactly what I needed.

Chapter 3

"Losers Never Win"

I called Norris to confront him about the other day and the situation he put Armani and I in. That was some bullshit. She could have gotten hurt, being caught up in the middle of all that mess, but he didn't answer. That's normally what he did when he fucked up and wanted to let passing time fix his problems.

If he didn't call back immediately to get into your head or give you some soft-ass story to try and manipulate you, he waited days before calling back, hoping you would forget what happened while he played it off as if it never happened. I didn't bother leaving a voicemail or texting him; instead, I hung up and let it go.

My phone rang back almost immediately, and it was Norris.

"Hello," I answered, but he didn't say anything. All I heard was noise.

"Hello," I said, again, but he still didn't say anything.

The noise was faint. Apparently, he pocket-dialed me and didn't know it. I could tell from the sound of the phone moving around in his pocket, as the material rubbed against the mouthpiece of the phone. I started to hang up, but something told me not to. I sat there and listened as hard as I could. I listened for about a minute and a half before the phone got clear enough for me to understand.

I heard a female's voice. She was saying, "Go to your baby mama, I know y'all still fucking around! I'm not doing this with you! Why are you still calling and texting her, if you don't want her anymore? Answer that!"

I couldn't tell who the person was. Then, I heard Norris telling the female, "No, baby, we're not fucking! I love you and only you. Please, don't go!"

The female responded, "Fuck that baby, Norris! If that's what you want, I can give you one. We can have our own."

When she said that, I got angry. I was Norris' only baby mama. I didn't know this chick or what I did to her to make her talk shit about me and my kid. Why was everyone thinking I still wanted Norris? I kept listening to the nonsense they were talking about, only to find out the entire time I was listening to the harshness of my sister, Michelle.

"Don't talk about my fuckin' baby! Watch your mouth! I've told you about that before," Norris replied.

"You're always taking up for them. I'm tired of this shit," Michelle hollered.

"Go, then! Fuck it! You always start this jealous shit," Norris hollered.

With my phone on mute, I laughed loudly at her mad-ass. She talked about my baby and I, only to get put in her place. It was funny that she was concerned about Norris and I's relationship and the fact that we were still communicating. She was threatened by me. She was jealous. She wanted a bigger title than she held. She wished she had a kid by him. She wanted what I had.

She couldn't stand my guts and I loved it. I wondered if I should contact Norris more to irritate her. I even thought about being around him more to keep her wondering where we were or what we were doing. There was so much I could do that I hadn't been... All for the sake of my relationship.

She could have Norris! I didn't want his ass anymore! Us fucking was a mistake anyway. Me getting pregnant by him was a mistake too. The abortion happened for a reason, and looking back now, I understand what took me to do it in the first place. Not knowing that I would turn around and get pregnant by him for a second time. I love my daughter, but I never planned for this kid to be his. Norris giving me her was the best thing he had ever done to and for me.

I couldn't believe how hard Michelle was coming for my daughter. I knew she hated me, but I didn't know how much she hated my daughter too. My own damn sister. It all started to sink in. Maybe it was because she was jealous of me the entire time - ever since we were kids. The signs were there, but once again, I ignored them, giving her the benefit of the doubt.

As the months went by, the time came for Chanel and I to head to court. With all the bullshit I dealt with, months went by quicker than I realized. The back-and-forth Chanel and I did over the money she stole, was finally coming to an end. I didn't care about sending her to jail, I just wanted my money. Once I got what was owed to me, it would be over for the two of us. I knew a friendship wouldn't stand a chance, after all she'd done.

When we went to court, Daddy went with me. Chris was with Chanel, as I expected. Chanel mugged me, periodically, which I wasn't threatened by. Chris peeped at me, just as he did when we were at Gracie's baby shower, almost the entire time we were in the courtroom. I didn't know if he was jealous that Anthony's fine-ass now sat next to me instead of him, or if he was checking my bad-ass out.

As usual, my hair was slayed, face was beat, and body was bangin'. I didn't have much body to flaunt, but what I did have, I managed to show off. My push-up bra was everything, my titties were sitting nice, my bandage dress hugged my curves and my stilettos had me standing like a stallion. After all the heartbreak and depression I went through, I can admit, I looked the best I had in a long time. I was glowing with happiness and peace and I knew neither of them could stand it.

I was nervous as hell to be in a courtroom; it was someplace I had never stood before. With the determination to win and get back what belonged to me, I loosened up a little.

"Everything will be alright, you can do it," My attorney said.

"Yeah, I'm good. We are gonna win. Now, let's go fight," I told him back.

We fought hard. With all the evidence we had, we won the case. I couldn't do it without my team, who'd been there since day one: Daddy, Gracie and my attorney. The judge demanded that Chanel pay me the entire $20,000, with the option of a payment plan or jail time if she refused to abide by the court's rules.

She was angry as hell. We had evidence it was her. The truth was right in front of us, but she still pretended to be innocent. She cussed and hollered, after walking out of the courtroom. Chanel was being the ghetto bitch she's always been, but none of that frightened me. I smiled and kept it cute, as I always did. There was no need for me to be upset. That's what happens when you do people dirty. Karma comes back to bite you in the ass. It's life. She was getting what she deserved. She may have thought she had gotten over on me, but she was now getting what she had coming to her.

While Chanel's lawyer pulled her aside to calm her down, Chris walked over to me and Daddy and said, "Here! Take this and just leave us the fuck alone."

Daddy looked at him like he was crazy for talking to me like that. He stared him down, as if he wanted to say or do some things that he couldn't do. Meanwhile, I stood there, unbothered by any of that, and opened the envelope. Shockingly, it was a $20,000 check.

"Daddy, look," I whispered to him.

"What?" He asked.

"It's a check! Chris paid his bitch's debt."

"Good! Now, we can leave these fucks alone before somebody gets hurt."

"Gets hurt? Why? It's not that serious," I told him.

It shocked me that he would give up so much money for her so soon in their relationship. They hadn't been dealing with each other that long, or had they? It made me wonder.

He did nice things for me when we started talking, but I'd never expected him to give me that much money so soon, or even put up that much money for me to give to someone else. The way he bent over backwards for her was cute. Since I could remember, her money-hungry-ass was dying to get with a ballin'-ass nigga like him. What she failed to understand was that nigga was psychotic. No amount of money in the world was worth putting up with the shit that came with him.

She saw the life I lived with him and wanted that badly, but there were some things I didn't tell her... Like the time he came in drunk one night and beat my ass. Or how much of an alcoholic he was, and how he changed from the guy I met shortly after... How he manipulated me into thinking he was a good man. And how he put everything and everyone else before me.

She was an outsider, looking in, not knowing all the shit I had to go through before becoming strong enough to walk away. She thought I was living a fairytale with him. Soon, she would find out what it's really like dating a guy who looked seemingly good on the outside, who spoiled her with the finer things but was mentally ill and difficult to deal with in reality.

No amount of money is worth being physically, emotionally and mentally abused. No diamond is worth dealing with someone that degrades you. No car or house is worth being controlled by a guy who claims to love you. Knowing your worth is worthiness. Being able to stand for everything you deserved and not falling for anything was better than all of that.

See, Chanel dealt with nothing but petty hustlers and broke niggas. She always thought I had a better life than she would ever have. If she could switch places with me, she would. The difference between me and her was, I was willing to bring her to the level where I was, or even higher. But Chanel would leave me at the bottom to make herself feel superior.

She always needed validation from other people to feel beautiful. She flaunted her body to guys to find love. She downed others to feel confident. So, the fact that she was dating my husband was no surprise to me.

Chapter 4

"Stalker"

Maybe about a week after we went to court, I started noticing some strange activity. I was getting blocked calls damn near every day. Someone was following me in a car I had never seen before. I even noticed the car sitting outside my house and outside the boutique, numerous times. It went on for about a week before I mentioned it to Daddy.

When I finally told him about it, he was pissed off at me for keeping it from him for so long. He was also worried about what the hell was going on and who it could be. Daddy was concerned about baby girl and I being in danger. He wasn't worried about himself much because he had a gun he carried everywhere with him. If it came down to him using it, he didn't have a problem with that either.

I had so many people against me, it was hard to narrow down or pinpoint who this suspicious person could actually be. I stayed away from the boutique and didn't take baby girl to the sitter for a while. I called the sitter to make sure she was ok and that she didn't notice anything strange. I concluded that maybe they were only after me.

Daddy stayed with us almost every day he could to make sure we were protected. As time went on, I started to really worry. This suspicious stalker was not letting up. My family and I could be in serious danger. Protecting us was my main priority. Daddy wouldn't be around every second of the day, so on Daddy's day off, I told him I wanted to get a gun.

At first, he looked at me crazy because he knew I wasn't that type of chick. Tara with a gun in her hand was unreal. I couldn't believe those words were actually coming out of my mouth.

From the first day he moved in and I saw his, he knew how much I always hated guns. I gave him so much shit about it because I never wanted one around. I never cared to shoot one, look at one or buy one. I was very ignorant when it came to guns and how they even worked; but there I was, on the way to the gun shop to purchase my very own. With this crazy-ass stalker, I really had no choice.

When we got to the gun shop, I looked at a few, small handguns that I thought I would be able to handle. Ones that didn't have too much power but would get the job done. The salesman showed me a few. I even held some, but they weren't the one. We spent almost an hour in the store, looking for the right one.

Then, I saw a pretty, pink, semi-automatic SIG Sauer P238. It was beautiful. I held it in my hands, and it sat perfectly. When I cocked it back, it slid smoothly, and it wasn't too difficult for me. I fell in love!

"This is the one, Daddy! This is the one," I told him, excitedly.

"Yeah, that's a nice one. It's perfect for you. If that's what my baby wants, then that's what she gets," Daddy told me.

"Sounds like you are one lucky lady," the salesman said to me.

"I am," I bragged, smiling back at him.

When we left the gun shop, Daddy drove me straight to the gun range. I was excited about having the gun because of how beautiful it was, but I wasn't sure if I was ready to shoot it. We spent hours in there, while Daddy showed me how to hold the gun properly, reload it and keep control while shooting. I began to get more comfortable. The sound no longer intimidated me, and by the time I left, I didn't feel like the amateur I was when I first walked through those doors.

The very next day, Daddy left Armani and I in the house. He felt comfortable enough now that he knew what I had and how to handle it. That day, nothing seemed out of the ordinary. There were no strange cars outside the house, no unknown numbers called me, and even things at the boutique were ok. I thought things were getting back to normal.

A week went by without any of the suspicious activity. Daddy and I were heading to his house because we were going to meet a realtor. After driving two miles, I noticed the same car, again, that followed me before. I was driving, and Daddy was in the passenger seat.

"Daddy," I said, in a warily voice.

"What's wrong, baby?"

"Look back! There's that car I was telling you about."

I looked in the rearview mirror, constantly, while Daddy turned back, periodically.

"At the next light, make a right. When you get to the stop sign, sit for a minute," Daddy told me, as he reached in the glove box to grab his gun.

I didn't know where it would lead us or what was about to happen, but I didn't bother asking either. I just did as I was told.

When I made the right at the light, the car did so as well. When I stopped at the stop sign, the car was right behind us. It was still difficult for me to see who was driving. I fixed my mouth to ask Daddy what to do next, but he said, "Sit here, I'll be back," as he hopped out the car.

He approached the car on the driver's side, while the hand that held the gun was behind his back. I was still in the car, looking at what was going on. I was not taking my eyes off Daddy for one second. I was scared, I couldn't believe what he was doing. I sat in the car, shaking my leg, and then I couldn't take it anymore, and hopped out the car too, going to the passenger door.

Daddy looked at me with a flustered look.

"Get back in the car," he yelled.

I shook my head no and proceeded to the car.

Daddy knocked on the window for the person to roll it down. While Daddy waited, I peeked in the passenger window. When I looked up, Daddy had his gun pointed at the person in the driver's seat. I yelled loudly, and as fast as I could, "Don't shoot, don't shoot; it's Chris!" Daddy looked at me, and then looked back at the car window. His gun was still drawn, ready to empty the clip.

Chris got out of the car, leaned on it and laughed at Daddy. I had never seen Daddy so upset. The entire time, it was only Chris. I'm sure the unknown calls were from him as well. I didn't understand his purpose, though. We both had clearly moved on and we both had an understanding that things were completely over for us. We were in the middle of getting divorced, so I didn't understand.

Daddy put the safety back on and put the gun in his pants. He stood in the middle of the street, in front of Chris, with his arms crossed for about two minutes before grabbing Chris by the shirt.

"So, it's been you harassing my family? I'm going to tell you this, one time only, stay away from my fuckin' family," Daddy told Chris.

"You don't have to tell me shit. I'm a grown-ass man and I do as I please, playboy. Now, let me go!"

"Or what? Come on! Hit me like you hit Tara!" Daddy said.

As I watched them both, I panicked. Chris had that demon inside of him! Daddy was in a rage. Being that he had his gun on him, I could see this ending badly. As I ran towards them to tell Daddy to calm down and get in the car, Chris knocked Daddy in the face, leaving him stumbling and holding his lip. Daddy got back up and rushed Chris to the ground. He got on top of him and continuously pounded him in the face.

Cars started pulling over. I heard one lady yell, "I'm calling the cops." A few guys got out their cars to break them apart.

"Daddy, come on," I yelled, as I tugged on his shirt.

"Hurry, let's go," I continued.

"This isn't over," Chris hollered.

Forgetting that we had a meeting with the realtor, we got in the car and headed back home.

Chapter 5

"Something That Disappoints"

When I woke up, Daddy was gone. I looked at my phone and I had a message from both him and Norris. Daddy's text said, "If you wake up and see this before I get back, I just want you to know that I ran out and got breakfast for all of us. I'll be back soon. Love you."

I didn't respond to Daddy's text; I opened the one from Norris. I hadn't spoken to him in a while. What was it now? Norris was unpredictable! If it wasn't one thing with him, it was another. Life with Norris was like living a terrible nightmare I couldn't shake.

The message read, "Tara, call me ASAP! This is very important! Please, call me when you get this!"

It sounded very important, and while Daddy was gone, I called Norris before he came back.

"Hey! What's up?"

"Yes, Norris, what do you want now?" I said, rolling my eyes.

"We really need to talk! I hope you won't be mad at me, after I tell you this!"

"What is it, Norris? Just say it! I don't have time for your mind games!"

"Tara, this isn't a joke!"

"Well... what?"

The phone got silent and I began to worry more.

"What is it, Norris?" I repeated.

"I just left the doctor."

"And? What does that have to do with me?" I asked.

"Well...well... I got tested and I was positive for chlamydia."

My mouth dropped! I hopped up in the bed and asked him to repeat himself.

"Say what now, Norris? Hold on! Say that again."

He got quiet on the phone and then said, "Man, somebody gave me chlamydia."

My heart was pounding in my chest. I hadn't been to the doctor since I started fucking with him. All I could think about was Daddy! If I had this shit, how would I explain this to Anthony? He didn't know I fucked Norris. I was in some deep shit. I had to get tested ASAP!

"Hello," Norris said, hesitantly.

"Tara," he went on.

"Nooo, Norris! How? How could you do this to me? How," I cried.

"I don't know how long I had it, Tara. I love you enough to tell you this, so you can get yourself checked. I would never give you something like that on purpose!"

I hung up on him. The possibility of having a STD scared the hell out of me. Especially, from someone I had no business fucking in the first place. I should have never done it. Norris has been messy from the first time I messed around with him. He dealt with anything that had a pussy. He didn't give a fuck, as long as he got his nut off. My stupid-ass knew that from the beginning. I should have known better than to mess around with his nasty-ass.

Daddy was off, and I had plans to lay up with him, watch some movies and just relax. While he was out, grabbing breakfast, I got dressed. I felt really bad about not being able to spend time with him, but I didn't have plans to be gone for long.

He got back before I could leave. He came back in the house with my favorite - IHOP. He knew how much I loved those buttermilk pancakes. I didn't even care how good that Big Steak Omelet smelled, how tender and well-seasoned that steak was, or even how soft and fluffy those pancakes were. After what Norris told me, I no longer had an appetite.

"Baby?" Daddy yelled from the kitchen.

"In here!" I yelled from the bathroom.

He was shocked to see me dressed and ready to head out, when we had plans to kick it.

"I thought we was chillin' today! Where are you headed?" He asked.

"I got a call from the boutique, so I'm gonna swing by and see what's going on. I won't be gone long…I promise!" I told him, as I kissed him on the lips.

"You don't mind keeping Mani, do you?" I asked.

He said, "Ok, we will be right here," and went on eating breakfast and playing with baby girl. I kissed her and Daddy goodbye and ran out the door. I felt so damn bad about lying, but there was no way I could tell him what Norris told me. If I didn't have it, then Daddy couldn't have it either. I didn't want to say more than I needed to. If I did test positive, then that was a different story that I would have to tell. For now, my mouth was sealed shut.

When I got to the office, it was packed. I was as nervous as could be. I was ashamed and embarrassed. Never did I think I'd be sitting in the doctor's office for this reason. I went in, did what I needed to do and left. They told me it would be at least 48 hours before I would be contacted. Whether good or bad, they would call to let me know.

The thought of having it changed my entire mood. I didn't want to do anything, but I still had to act like myself when I went back home, so I wouldn't alert Daddy that something was wrong. It was the worst thing ever. I was such a hypocrite. I never wanted to keep anything from him. My previous relationship turned out to be a disaster for that same reason.

When I got back, Daddy asked me how things went at the boutique. With a puzzled look on my face, I started thinking, *what the hell is he talking about.* I almost blew my cover, but then I immediately snapped back.

"Oh, everything's good now! Just had some confusion with inventory."

"Glad it wasn't bad, baby, and you got things squared away."

I gave him a hug and a kiss, and we went in the bedroom and laid across the bed. Baby girl fell asleep on my chest, so I went and laid her down in her bed. When I came back, Daddy was laying on the bed, looking at the ceiling.

"What's wrong?" I asked. He didn't answer, as if he didn't hear me speaking to him.

"Has Chris been following or contacting you, since the other day?" Daddy asked.

"No! He has actually backed off. Maybe that ass whipping was what he needed," I joked. Daddy agreed, as we both laughed about it.

He got on top of me and started kissing and rubbing my titties, but I wasn't in the mood. He could tell I didn't feel like it. Normally, I would get real nasty with him, but I thought about everything that happened today and it turned me off instantly.

Normally, as soon as he touched me, I would be wet like Aquafina and dripping like a faucet, but I couldn't fuck him, thanks to Norris. I didn't know if I had that shit. There was no way in hell I could give it to Daddy, if I did. He would catch it for sure because we didn't use protection.

"What's wrong, baby?" Daddy asked.

Yawning, I said, "I'm just tired. This was my day to relax and I still wasn't able to. I'm sorry, Daddy, not tonight."

Days went by and I waited on that phone call. I was tempted to call the office to make sure that they didn't forget to call me. The very next day, after I was going to call them, they called me. I was beyond nervous. I was shaking from the time I answered the phone, anxious to hear the news, but scared as hell.

"Good afternoon. I'm trying to reach Mrs. Anderson. Is she available?" The nurse asked.

"This is her," I replied.

"Well, we got your results back from your STD testing, which included chlamydia, gonorrhea, syphilis and HIV. I just wanted to let you know that everything was negative!"

I went silent, closed my eyes and I immediately thanked God. I prayed about those results. I almost forgot that I was on the phone.

"Hello? Mrs. Anderson? Are you still there?"

"Yes…I'm sorry. Thank you so much for getting back to me!"

"No problem. If you have any questions or concerns, please feel free to call the office. Do you need the number?"

"No, ma'am, I have it. Thanks, again."

"Have a great afternoon, Mrs. Anderson."

"You too!" I told the nurse and hung up.

Damn! Look at God; He was definitely on my side. Norris and I did use a condom, but shit, things still can happen. It was better to be safe than sorry. Now that I knew I was clear, I knew that Daddy was too…unless he had been fucking around. I knew I didn't have shit, so if he ever fixed his mouth to tell me the same shit Norris did, we definitely would have some issues.

By the next day, I was back to my normal self. Daddy looked at me crazy because for the past few days I had been mopping around. He didn't question me, though; he hardly ever did. The majority of the time, he rolled with the flow. He knew I had a little bit of crazy in me. He saw early on that I could be a psychotic bitch. Maybe he didn't speak on certain things to keep the peace; and that, I was fine with.

I had already been there and done that. I was controlled, I was questioned and abused. I was done with all of that. I found strength to walk away from that toxic situation, and no way in hell was I going to deal with that again. I liked the man he was. I loved how he handled things and how he let me do as I pleased to fulfill my own happiness. Don't get me wrong, he did a lot to make me happy too, but dealing with a man that didn't control me, question me or make assumptions was heaven-sent. Not too many of those kinds floated the streets these days.

Daddy left out to go to work. I stayed home, cleaning. I had my music blasting, dancing around the house and I lit some candles. I was feelin' myself. Everything was good. Then, my phone rang. It was from an unknown number, again. *Why the hell was Chris calling me blocked, if I knew who he was already and that it was him all along?* I thought. When I answered, he hung up. I knew for sure it was Chris, so I called him.

"Chris?! Why are you still calling me blocked?" I asked, angrily.

"I didn't call you!"

"Well, who was it then?"

"How the hell would I know, Tara?"

"OK… well…"

"Wait! Tara? Can I talk to you for a second?"

"About what? There is nothing to talk about, Chris!"

"Man, I didn't mean to freak you out, I was just trying to get yo' attention. I miss you! I really wish we could work things out again."

"You don't stand a chance. You really thought we could come back from you fucking a bitch I once called a friend and loved as a sister? Really, Chris? You must be out yo' damn mind! Now, like Anthony said, stay away from me, lose my number and I'll see you in court!" I said, right before hanging up on him.

Arguing with Chris made me forget everything I had going on. If it wasn't Chris, who the hell was it this time? Chanel wasn't the type to call blocked. She would let it be known that it was her. I sat on the counter, thinking. As I sat there, my phone rang, again. It was the blocked number. I decided to answer it, again, to see if I could figure out who it was.

"Hello?" I answered the call, with an attitude.

"Wow, Tara, you really can't stay away from my man! I knew you still wanted him. You have a man and still feel the need to fuck mine. You just have to be a greedy bitch, don't you?" Michelle argued.

I couldn't believe it was her. I hadn't spoken to her in the longest time. I thought she forgot my number.

"Listen, bitch! I don't give a fuck about you or Norris, ok? Newsflash, bitch, I've had him and if I still wanted him, I could get him back. I could hurt your feelings so badly right now, but I'm not going to be a bitter bitch. Besides, you're already miserable. I don't want Norris and I damn sure don't want his infected dick. Now, instead of calling my line with all this bullshit, how about you call a clinic to get checked? You wanted my leftovers so badly, well… now, he has you burning and didn't even bother telling you. Girl, bye!"

It was obvious Norris didn't tell her shit about what he had going on. She was on the phone speechless. Clearly, I hit a nerve with the things I said. I had no sympathy for her, though. That backstabbing bitch didn't care about me when she started fucking with Norris, so she deserved everything she had coming to her. Dealing with Norris was never a walk in the park. She knew that. She knew what I went through with that jackass, but he was her headache now. While she was miserable and getting treated like I once did, I was on the other side of town, living my *almost* best life.

Chapter 6

"Better Be Careful"

I had been so caught up in bullshit and unnecessary drama, that I hadn't seen or spoken to Gracie in a while. I had to check on them and go over to visit Gracelyn. I suggested we meet up and do lunch, so we met at a Mexican restaurant. I really missed having her at the boutique and talking to her. I knew she was busy with work and was now planning a wedding that I could not wait for.

When we got to the restaurant, we sat down and started talking about everything. She brought up Chanel and Chris and asked how things were since we went to court for the money. She had no idea what I went through after all that, so I told her.

"Girl! Where do I begin? Chris was more of the problem after that, believe it or not. I was expecting some bullshit from Chanel, but I haven't seen or heard from her. She has been laying low, lately!" I told Gracie.

"I wonder why. That's strange. Not the turn up queen," Gracie joked.

"I don't know. It is strange, though. Let me tell you about her partner. So, I had this strange car I had never seen before following me for about two weeks, if not a little longer. The car sat in front of the house, sat outside the boutique and followed me multiple times a week. I even had blocked numbers calling me and they called over and over again. Whenever I did decide to answer the phone, there would be complete silence and then they would hang up. It got so bad that I told Anthony about it and he refused to leave baby girl and I alone. We even went to get me a gun, girl, and I went to the gun range to learn how to use it. I did tell you Anthony decided to sell the house after his grandma passed, right? "

"Yeah, you told me," Gracie said.

I continued, "Ok, so we were on our way to Anthony's house one day and the car was like one car behind us, following us. I was driving, and when I noticed it in the rearview mirror, I told Anthony. Only God knows how long the car had been following us, but I didn't realize it until we got almost by the Wendy's on Main Street."

"No way! So, what did y'all do? Was baby girl with y'all?" Gracie asked.

"No, she wasn't with us, thank God. It gets better. So, Anthony told me to pull over and sit at the stop sign, and sure enough, the car followed. I was so scared. Anthony grabbed his gun, got out the car and went up to the damn mysterious car!"

"What? Who was it? What happened?"

"Shortly after he got out, I got out behind him. He went to the driver's side and I went to the passenger side. I peeked in the window, and girl, it was Chris the entire time. When I looked up, Anthony had his gun drawn, ready to shoot."

"Did he shoot him? Did you call the police at all? "

"I didn't. I should have. I didn't think about that. I wanted to know who it was, more than anything. No, Anthony didn't shoot. Thankfully, he ended up putting the gun down, but they did end up fighting, though... In the middle of the street. Some guys got out their cars and broke it up. A lady threatened to call the police, so I grabbed Anthony and we sped off; but when we were leaving, Chris yelled to Anthony that it wasn't over. Whatever that meant."

"I hope Chris doesn't do anything crazy for retaliation. I don't need him dragging Josh into none of his bullshit and putting everyone's life in danger. It was his fault that all of that happened anyway," Gracie said.

"Yeah, you're right about that."

"So, why was he following you in the first place?"

"We ended up talking and he told me he was trying to get my attention. All to ask me something I turned down."

"Let me guess, he wanted to sleep with you again?" Gracie asked.

"No! Well, maybe that question would have come eventually, but he wanted to know if we could work things out."

"Is he still dealing with Chanel?"

"Girl, I have no idea, but I mentioned that situation and asked if he was out of his damn mind. Never would I ever deal with Norris or Chris again."

"Well, you know what they say, 'You never know what you have until it's gone.' I guess he's realizing it now."

"You're right about that."

"Speaking of Norris," Gracie said, shaking her head.

I sat there, listening to her, with nothing to say. I was curious to know what she knew about him. There was no way I was telling her what went on with us. She didn't know I fucked him at his place. She didn't know about me going for the STD testing either. That was way too much information for her anyway, so I kept it quiet. When she mentioned Norris, I just rolled my eyes and sat there, waiting for her to spill the tea. I was certain I knew the topic she would bring up anyway.

"What about this nigga?" I asked Gracie, as if I knew nothing about what he had going on.

"Between me and you, Josh told me that he has, or had, chlamydia and God knows what else. Apparently, when he found out, it was too late for Michelle and she caught it too."

I raised my eyebrows and drank my margarita. When I said that to her on the phone, I didn't know she had it for sure. I was just being petty and wanted to make her mind wander, but I knew she had it coming. To see her life crumbling was crazy. She was starting to get shit back worse than she gave it.

"No, Gracie, you're lying!"

"I wish I could say I was."

"So, clearly, one of them has to be messing around. I wonder which one of them it was," I replied.

"You know Norris is a ho," Gracie said.

"Hell, Michelle is too! There's no telling who brought that nasty shit on to the next person. It could have been me dealing with all of that, Gracie." I shook my head. "Thankfully, I dodged that bullet."

"Let me tell you. Your life is dandelions and roses, ok? I know you're dealing with a lot and it's always so much at once, but just remember, it could have been worse. Behind every struggle is a blessing. You are on your way to greatness. There is a light at the end of the tunnel, but you have to be the one to push through in order to see it."

I sat there and just listened. I took in everything Gracie said. I needed that reminder and motivation she gave me. I had come this far, I knew I could go further, but at times I disbelieved.

"Thank you so much. You don't understand how much I needed to hear that," I told Gracie, while hugging her and kissing all over her cheeks.

"I forgot to ask you how Norris was with baby girl. Is he doing as he promised?" Gracie asked.

"Girl... My life is a mess, ok? There's a story behind that too. I don't know if I told you that I did go and meet him at his place that time after I called you about it, but I did. He told me he wanted to talk and wanted me to bring her with me, so they could have some playing and bonding time. That's why he wanted me to come over to talk versus speaking over the phone. When I got there, it was more than the three of us. Michelle and Chanel were there as well. Norris never told me that they would be there; so, there the three of us were, arguing and about to fight in front of my damn child, Gracie. What if she had gotten hurt? Norris doesn't think. Well… about anybody else except himself. I am so over him and his shit. My gut was telling me to leave, but I didn't listen. His mediation session only made it worse between us."

"Oh, yeah, let me tell you this too. Please, be careful around him. Keep your distance, if you can. Word around town is that he's selling more dope. He also messed up with some big-time dealers and did them dirty. They want him dead. I've told Josh he can talk to him on the phone, but going out with him, going over to his place, and running the streets with him ain't gon' cut it. Josh has finally left that mess alone and he's working a good job now. I can't lose him to the streets over his homeboy's B.S. I can't, Tara," Gracie cried.

"Listen, Josh is much wiser than Norris. I knew he was only in the streets because he had to be. Y'all are gonna be alright. We are all gonna be alright. I hardly be around Norris anyway because it's always something with him. Don't worry!" I told her.

"This conversation was so deep; I didn't have time to play with my Gracelyn," I continued.

"I know! It's ok. We'll meet up again soon and bring the kids back together, so they can actually move around and play next time."

"Definitely," I replied.

When I left her, I went back home. When I got home, Daddy told me that he finally sold the house. It wasn't a huge house and it was quite old, but he was able to get $75,000 for it. We were sitting on so much money, I started to consider opening another boutique. Then, I thought about the pressure and stress it would bring. You would think a young bitch with money would be happy as hell, but it didn't turn out like that.

I even thought about buying another house. I hated living in condos sometimes. I wanted my baby to be able to go outside and run around in a big-ass yard, while I sat my sexy-ass in the sun, drinking piña coladas. Buying another house with another man gave me anxiety, though, with all the shit I had to go through when I parted ways with Chris.

"I love you so much. You mean everything to me. There is nothing in this world I wouldn't do for you. I want you to look for a new house. Whatever you want! Wherever you want!" Daddy told me.

"You deserve so much more than what I'm able to give you right now, but soon all of that will change," he continued.

He was so sweet. It was the little things that mattered... like the notes he left, the texts he sent throughout the day, and him calling to check on me - multiple times - when he was gone. He always seemed to know what I wanted and what to say at the right times. Listening to everything he said, instantly, changed my mind about us buying a place together. He was different, and he showed me. I wasn't understanding why I wasn't treating him like he was. This man was good to me.

We had been living together for more than six months now. Everything was perfect. We didn't have any issues. It was nice having him around. Buying a place with him was something I didn't think I would regret. This was the one, y'all. He was the one for me. Losing all the guys I did in the past was worth it. Anthony is my everything.

Chapter 7

"Just a Little Jealousy"

Norris called me out the blue. He did that a lot. He would call one day, and then wait weeks before calling again. He wasn't consistent. I didn't know if it was because he was so caught up in the streets or if he wasn't concerned much about our kid. I didn't want to believe he wasn't because he showed lots of love to her, when he did call or come around.

"Hey, Tara"

"Hey, Norris. What's up?"

"I wanted to check on my baby. What she doing? I miss her!"

"Oh, she's just sitting on this floor, playing with her toys. You don't hear all that damn noise she's makin'?"

Norris laughed. "That's my girl. I miss her a lot. I need to see her soon."

"Well, I'm not coming over there again. You fucked that up the last time I brought her over."

"I was just trying to make things better, man."

"You should have told me. What if things went left and some shit popped off? Let me just remind you, it was close to happening. You put my child in harm's way, keeping me in the dark about all that was happening. That was fucked up!"

"I know, man, I know! I didn't think about all that."

"Clearly!"

"Well, when can I see her?"

"I don't know!"

"What you mean?"

"Exactly what I said! I'm not coming there, and I need to check with my nigga to see how he feels about you coming here."

"Why can't we meet somewhere?"

"Like where?"

"The park or something, I don't know."

"That's possible."

"Norris, where the fuck you at?" I heard in his background. It sounded like Michelle and she sounded angry. I knew she hated him talking to me, so that was expected. I didn't know how this shit was gonna work with him having to co-parent with me and dating my sister - who I hated.

"I'm in the room!" He yelled back.

"Hold on, Tara!" Norris told me.

I could hear him sitting the phone down. My nosy-ass sat there on hold too, listening to their conversation and eating popcorn, as if I was watching my favorite Lifetime movie. That's what their relationship reminded me of, anyway. It felt damn good to be on the other side, knowing I wasn't the one dealing with his bullshit anymore. Daddy was gone, out of town, and baby girl was sleep; so, I had lots of free time to sit on the phone as long as I wanted.

"You are full of shit!" Michelle said.

"What the fuck are you talking about now?" Norris asked her.

"I went through your phone last night and saw you texting a bitch! Telling her you love her, and you can't wait to see her! Now, who is it?"

"Man, you trippin'!"

"No, nigga, you trippin'!"

"Get off my shirt, girl! Let me go! Put my shit down!"

"You got to be the stupidest nigga to cheat with an unlocked phone."

"Give me my shit!" Norris hollered at Michelle.

"Who the fuck is this?"

"Girl, you know what I use that phone for, so what you think?"

Norris always had two phones because he was in the streets. He never gave his customers his personal number he gave people he actually fucked with.

"Well, call the number then! Call it!" She told him.

I was still sitting on hold, trying my hardest to hear every single word being said. Their voices sounded some distance away, so that made it difficult for me to hear, but I was still trying.

"Put it on speaker!" Michelle continued.

The phone rang and rang, as if the person he was calling wasn't going to pick up, but then they did.

"Hello?" The female said on the phone. The chick who answered the phone was Allie, Michelle's best friend she's had since like elementary. She was one of Michelle's roommates before she moved in with Norris. When I heard that, I shuffled around to hear better, causing some of my popcorn to fall on my lap.

"Allie?" Michelle yelled.

"Yes?" Allie replied.

"Do you know who this is?"

"Yes!" Allie continued.

"What the fuck are you doing textin' my dude?"

"Check yo' nigga not me! The person you need to be questioning is Norris. Real question is, what is he doing texting me?"

"That's some foul shit! You knew we were dealing! You knew that!"

"I did! I don't have an issue with that. You can have me too, if you want! Ain't like we ain't never had each other before. He's wanted a threesome with the two of us for a while now," Allie went on.

"Come over...shit!" Michelle told her.

"Hell yeah!" Norris yelled, right after Allie hung up.

"See, baby! It all worked out. We can all have each other!" He continued.

"Norris, we can do the threesomes, but you better not ever fuck her or contact her without me being around or knowing."

"I got you, baby!" Norris told Michelle.

I heard Michelle tell Norris she was going to get in the shower before Allie got there, and he said ok. His voice was getting clearer, as if he was approaching the phone, so I hung up.

What the fuck was going on? This shit was a mystery and awkward as hell too. I never knew Allie and Michelle fucked around. I never knew either of them were into girls. Growing up, Michelle never showed interest in a woman. I didn't know who the hell she was anymore.

What I heard was so disgusting, I couldn't finish my popcorn. Damn! These bitches were really bowing down to Norris. Degrading themselves as a woman to make this fuckboy happy. Man, if Momma was alive, she would be so disappointed in Michelle right now.

After I got off the phone, I didn't have anything else to do. I did a few things around the house, but after that, I was bored, again. I tried finding some places to go, just to get out the house, but after living here all my life, nothing excited me. So, I ended up over at Gracie's, to hang out with her, Josh and Gracelyn for a while.

Josh answered the door and hugged baby girl and I. He grabbed Mani from me and took her to their kitchen to get snacks. He always gave the kids snacks and candy, and then left them with their moms for them to drive us crazy. We had a lot to talk about because Josh still didn't know that Norris and I took a DNA test and found out that she was his friend's kid, instead of his brothers.

So, we all sat in the living room, talking, while the kids played beside us. We started drinking and playing Uno. We were having a really good time.

"Man, listen, Josh, I really appreciate the love you show baby girl and I. We really appreciate you," I told him.

"Oh, no doubt! I know you and Chris going through y'all shit, but you forever family. That's my niece, man. That's how it's supposed to be."

"About that…" I started, as I put my head down a little.

"Well, she, technically, isn't your niece," I continued.

"What you mean?"

"Well, some shit happened, and Norris was a potential father, so we went to take the DNA test and it showed Norris is her dad."

"That's alright, sis. Shit, that's bro too, so she still my niece anyway. I don't give a damn about what any of y'all have going on. We all have been there for each other, since day one, and that's how it's gonna be. You still sis, that's still my niece and we are forever family," Josh said.

"Awww… y'all are giving me teary eyes," Gracie chimed in.

We all laughed.

"Man, that's crazy, though, 'cause I was just talking to Chris, saying how none of us had kids, and then out the blue we all dropped kids at the same time and now he's about to have two. He didn't correct me either. Do he know about the test?"

"He about to have two?" I asked Josh, with a puzzled look on my face.

"DAMN!" Josh yelled, as if he knew he fucked up.

"So, Chanel is pregnant?" I asked him.

He started shaking his head, looking at Gracie, as we both stared at him, waiting for an answer. Gracie didn't know that either. Maybe it was supposed to be a secret Chris asked Josh to keep, but it slipped out.

"I didn't mean to say that, man. Just don't tell nobody. So, yeah, they got a little one on the way."

Honestly, my feelings were slightly hurt. Yeah, we were going through with the divorce. Yes, we both had moved on, but I still had love for Chris and cared about him a little bit, no matter how much I tried to fight it and convince myself that I didn't.

When I started dealing with Anthony, it was to clear my mind from Chris and help me move on. I jumped into someone else with feelings and emotions still there for my past lover. When I loved someone, I loved hard. It was hard for me to move on. I never believed in unloving someone that once held my heart.

I love Daddy and I'm happy we ended up dealing with each other, but what we had was a different kind of love. I couldn't explain it. I still thought about Chris and cared what he had going on. I still felt a little bad about dealing with Daddy while still, technically, being married. I wasn't giving my all to him because of that, but Chris was out here getting bitches pregnant. It was hard for me to digest that. The baby that my so-called best friend was carrying was supposed to be our baby.

I sat there on the couch with nothing to say. Gracie and Josh could tell I was hurt. Josh got up and went upstairs. Gracie came over and hugged me, rubbed my back and told me everything was gonna be alright. I heard her voice, I felt her touch, but I was so gone, I didn't really hear or feel her much.

I got up and started gathering Mani's things. I grabbed Armani and told Gracie I was leaving. I didn't want to be around anyone. I didn't want to be bothered. My whole mood changed. The person I was when I walked in wasn't the same leaving out.

Gracie yelled, "Call me when y'all get home!"

I said, "Yeah," got in the car and Gracie stood in the door and watched as I pulled off.

I wasn't upset with her. I didn't want her to feel that way. I didn't mean to be rude, but I had so much on my mind. I didn't pay attention to how I spoke to her.

When I pulled off, I went up the street and came up to a stop sign. "Damn, damn, damn!" I yelled, as I shed a few tears and beat on my steering wheel. I sat at the stop sign for a few minutes, while horns honked at me and I wasn't even fazed.

I pulled off slowly, and then came to a stop light.

"Fuck Chris! Fuck Chanel! Fuck Norris! Fuck Michelle!" I told myself over and over again. I repeated it continuously, as I sat at the light.

"I don't know why I'm trippin' over these sorry-ass niggas!" I was always in my feelings about shit I could not control or change. "What the hell was wrong with me?" I asked myself.

I turned on the radio to ease my mind and *Karma* by Queen Naija was on. It was one of my favorite songs, so I started singing the chorus loudly.

I sung to the top of my lungs, feelin' the entire song, as I sung it. I swore she made that song about my life, 'cause I was damn near living those lyrics.

I raced home to get in the bathtub. I know it may sound crazy, but it helped to ease my mind and helped me focus. I wondered if he rubbed her belly and tended to her like he did me. I wondered if his face lit up when he found out like it did when I told him. I wondered if he would propose to her when she gave birth, as he proposed to me. I can't even lie; I was an emotional wreck. Sadly, it took me days to get it off my mind.

When I got home from the boutique, a few days later, Daddy was finally back from being gone for so long. I went to sit on the couch next to him while I hugged and kissed him, showing him how much I missed him. You know, I was trying to tend to my man and get some of his good loving I was overdue for. As soon as we were getting into it, my phone rung. Daddy looked at me and I looked at him.

"It's Norris," I told him.

"Are you going to answer it?"

"You might as well see what he wants. It's late. It might be important," he continued.

I picked the phone up.

"Yes, Norris? Why are you calling me this time of night?"

I heard a lot of noise in his background, but I couldn't tell what it was.

"Where you at?" He asked, breathing heavily, as if he had just finished running a marathon.

"Why? What's going on? What's wrong with you?"

"Man, please come by my spot."

"What is going on?"

"Man, yo' sister is going crazy."

"I don't have a sister," I said, being petty.

"What's going on with y'all, Norris?" I continued.

"She caught me and Allie fuckin'. Her and Allie was fighting, and I broke them up and got Allie out the house. Allie already left, but Michelle is in here trying to fight me and stab me now. She got those charges pending, so I don't want to call the police; and I don't want to beat her ass in here either, but I will have to if she doesn't chill out. Come get me."

"Listen, brah, that ain't my problem. I'm not getting in the middle of y'all shit! You're gonna have to figure this shit out on your own. That's yo' bitch, yo' side bitch and y'all problems... ain't got shit to do wit' me," I told him, and then I hung up.

Daddy was pissed. He was tired of Norris calling me for things that didn't involve our kid. He'd been trying his hardest lately to keep me away from him. I didn't know if he thought Norris would try me again, if he thought I would cheat on him and end up with Norris or if he just didn't like the dude. All I knew was, he hated him and didn't want me involved with him at all.

"Block his number!" Daddy said, sternly.

"I can't block him, Anthony! We have a kid!"

"Stop talking to him!"

"It's not like he was calling to get with me. He just wanted my help and I declined it. I'm being honest, so you're aware. I didn't want to keep anything from you! Calm down! I'm yours! My heart belongs to you!"

"What about that pussy?"

"It's yours too!" I said, blushing hard.

"Come in the room!"

I already knew what it was. My test came back negative, so I was good. I was ready to suck on him, get some head and throw these legs in the air, baby!

He dragged me in the room, pushed me down on the bed, took my pants off, pulled down my panties and dived right in. I was moaning loudly, screaming his name and being held from running, but Daddy kept going. I wrapped my arms around him, pulling him closer, wanting him to go deeper. I ran my nails across his back while he went deeper inside me. I moaned more and more from the pain and pleasure he gave me. It felt so damn good I didn't want him to stop. But then, he shot all his babies in me. After, we went to take a shower and then went sound asleep.

I knew he wasn't trippin' for no reason. He just needed me to put this pussy on him; give his fine-ass some "act right," as they called it. He couldn't go without having me for too long; and hell, I didn't blame him. Really, how could I, when the sex we had always blew his mind?

Chapter 8

"Yet Another Victim"

D addy hadn't seen his brothers since their grandma's funeral, so he went out to have some fun and spend some time with them.

"How was your night with your brothers?" I asked, when he got back.

"It was alright, but I have a lot to talk to you about."

"What happened? Is everything ok? You look concerned. You're scaring me! What is it about?" I asked.

"Them, Norris, Mani… and you."

I sat up in the bed and said, "Armani? They have never met her! How the fuck is she involved in anything?"

"Well, remember how I told you that I don't really fuck with my brothers like that because they run the streets?"

"Yeah!"

"Well, I found out a lot tonight. I thought we were meeting up at one of their cribs or a bar or something, but he changed the plans and texted me a different address. I wasn't going to go, but I went because I hadn't seen them in a while and life is short. You know? So, I went to spend some time with them. I was sitting in a fuckin' trap house."

"What does this have to do with my daughter?"

"Just chill, let me explain. So, we were all laughing, drinking, chillin', playing 2k19 and this guy came in. He works for one of my bros. He told him they had a problem and needed to talk to him. My bro refused to get up to talk and insisted that he speak right there in front of me. The dude was like, 'Yeah, Norris didn't show up to the meeting spot to pay us the money, and now we're looking for him.' My bro told the guy to handle that! I don't know what that means, but all I know is he doesn't play about his money. They are after Norris! You need to stay away from him before things turn out bad. You and baby girl could get caught up in it, if you don't!"

My eyes started to water. "Well, can't you tell them not to bother us?"

"It's not that easy. This man moves major weight. He will do what he has to in order to get what belongs to him. He turned on family and did them in… If you know what I mean. That's why I don't be around them. They move funny. They are too hot and that's bad for my image as a lawyer."

"Fuck!" I yelled, sitting in the middle of the bed, holding my head.

"It's gon' be alright. As long as you stay away from Norris."

"Do they know who we are? Me and Mani?" I asked.

"I don't think so. That's why it's important you stay away before they do find out," he repeated.

At that point, I was like fuck Norris! Our lives were in danger. If anybody asked, I didn't know the nigga. I wasn't going to get myself or my daughter caught up in anymore of his shit. All this was going on because he wanted to be in the streets he knew nothing about, and then became greedy with it. He was really fuckin' up with a lot of people. Now, he had fucked up with the wrong ones.

I wanted to call Norris. I wanted to ask him what all of this was about and warn him of what he had coming to him; but as bad as I wanted to, I couldn't. I didn't want him to end up dead. That was my child's father, for heaven sake. I couldn't explain this to Mani later on. I knew if anything happened, I would feel guilty for not warning him while I knew about it. All I did was pray. He needed angels over him.

It was getting late, so I laid back down to go to sleep. I slept closely to Daddy that night, since I was worried about what he told me. All I remember saying to myself before I fell asleep was, *I should have listened to Daddy a long time ago, and left Norris' ass alone like he said.*

Norris texted me the next day. I didn't respond. He called me many times, but I didn't answer. I didn't know what he was calling for and I didn't care. We weren't meeting up, I wasn't bringing my kid around him, I wasn't helping him get out of a hole he dug himself into, I didn't have any money for him, so there was no need to answer.

Gracie texted me to check on me too. This was another one of those times where I was busy with shit going on over on my end, that I didn't have much time for my friend. In fact, I hadn't talked to her since the other night I found out Chanel was pregnant by Chris.

When I hit her up, she apologized to me for everything, as if it was her fault. She wanted to be sure I was good. The chick had a heart of gold. She was nothing like them other bitches I hung with. That's one reason why I fucked with her so hard.

Focused on me and mines, I ended up blocking Norris' number. He would not stop calling and texting me. I wanted to leave him alone, this time, like Daddy told me. The heads up he gave me wasn't overlooked and I wanted to be sure he knew that. I wanted him to know I wasn't taking this matter lightly.

As I sat in the house, after getting off the phone with Gracie, I realized it had been a while since I went to the boutique. At that moment, I knew I'd been going through hell lately, because that wasn't like me. I decided to get cute, hit the mall to do some shopping and head over to the boutique to clear my mind. When I got there, I checked on the girls and brought them some lunch and Edible Arrangements, just to show them how much I appreciated them for keeping the place running smoothly.

I went and sat in my office for a while, doing paperwork, and making sure everything looked right and things were being handled properly. Then, I got a knock on the door. Chelsea, one of my shift managers, came in and asked me if I had a minute. She never talked to me alone, so I immediately thought something was wrong. When I had good folks standing behind me and helping me, I had all the time in the world for them - no matter how busy I was.

She came in, closed the door behind her and told me that a girl has been coming by the boutique, asking if I was there, for the past couple of days. That disturbed me. Who was this chick? Chelsea continued on and told me that she'd been trying to call me to let me know, but my phone was going to voicemail. That must have been around the time I had my phone on do not disturb for a couple days…right before I blocked Norris.

I asked her what the girl looked like. She explained that it was a short, thick, dark-skinned chick with lots of piercings, who wore burgundy weaves, crop tops and Jordan's all the time. I knew someone who matched that description, but it wasn't anybody I was close enough with to be coming and looking for me. Allie side-eyed me at Gracie's shower and didn't speak, so there was no reason for her to be looking for me. Why was she looking for me, after dealing with Norris and fighting with Michelle?

I thanked Chelsea for the heads up, and when she left out the office, I continued on with what I was doing. I wasn't worried, nor was I concerned. I sat in the office for about 45 minutes after talking to Chelsea, and then I got a text message from her. She said the girl she was telling me about was back again and was about to walk in the boutique. I texted her back and told her I would be right out.

As I exited the office and walked from the back, Allie was just walking in. She looked at me… I looked at her, curious to know why the hell she'd been coming there looking for me.

"Hey, Tara. I don't mean to bother you, but do you have a minute?" She asked.

I stood there, with my arms crossed and my back against the counter, thinking about what I should say. Should I tell her to leave because there was nothing to talk about? Should I give her the minute she asked for to hear her out and possibly get some tea? Hmm...decisions, decisions. My nosy-ass ended up giving her the time she asked for, to see what she had to say.

"Yeah, let's step outside," I told her.

"Thank you so much. I know we haven't spoken in a while, but I just want you to know I have nothing to do with what you and Michelle is going through. I have no beef with you."

"Well, let me ask you this... What was all that about at Gracie's baby shower?"

"I don't recall!" Allie said, acting dumb, like she had no clue what I was talking about.

"You walked in with Gina and gave me a side-eye. I was confused because I never had an issue with you."

"If I did, I apologize. Like I said, I don't have beef with you. However, if my friend doesn't fuck with certain people, I don't either, because my loyalty is with my friend."

"Ok, I get that! So, with that being said, Michelle and I haven't resolved our issues, so why are you here now?"

"Well, I wanted to talk to you because I need you."

When she said that, my eyes grew wide. It was funny how the people who fucked me over, did me dirty, or once hated me, now ran to me with their problems or needed me most. They would never forgive me like they expected me to forgive them. It was crazy!

"I don't know how I could possibly help you, but I'm listening," I told her.

"Well, Norris and I was messing around on the low."

When she said that, I immediately rolled my eyes and rejected her. Here goes some more shit with Norris and I'm trying to stay away from him and his problems.

"Uh… that ain't my problem! What you and Norris have going on is-"

I tried to explain, but she interrupted me.

"It's more to it than that, Tara! Just please, please, listen to me. I need your help," Allie begged.

"What is it?" I asked.

"I'm pregnant by Norris. Michelle doesn't know, and I don't know what to do," Allie cried.

"It wasn't supposed to be strings attached, but I love him. Now, I'm pregnant and he wants me to get an abortion. Look!" Allie continued.

She pulled out her phone, showing me the text messages between her and Norris. I read, "I don't need another baby right now! It's best to get rid of it! We can still be together! That was a mistake."

When she mentioned the abortion, I couldn't help but think about my experience and how it left me feeling. I wouldn't wish that on my worst enemy. It was her first kid and all I saw in her was myself ten years ago. I hugged her, although I didn't care for her too much.

"It's gonna be alright, girl! It's gonna be alright!" I told her.

"I just don't know what to do. He's pressuring me into killing an innocent baby! My first kid! I can't do that, Tara, but what if I don't? Will I be a single parent? That's not fair! He fathers your kid! Why can't he father mine?" Allie cried.

"What you fail to understand is, Norris and I had history. We were more than fuck friends, no offense! Norris is out here hoeing around, and you knew that. You caused this on yourself, boo. I can't make this decision for you. You have to make this on your own; because at the end of the day, you will be fully responsible for that child's life - with or without Norris!" I preached.

"He told me he loved me!"

"But he's also fucking with your best friend and she had him before you, so why believe that? I'm sure he tells every chick he bangs that he loves them. Why would you believe him?"

"I don't know! This wasn't supposed to happen!"

"Well, this is something you need to sit down and discuss with him, not me, honestly! If you end up keeping the kid, I would like to stay in contact with you, as our kids will be siblings. I need to tell you something, though. Be careful around Norris because I've heard some things and his name stinks in these streets."

"What do you mean?" Allie asked, with a worried look on her face.

"That's all I can say." I gave her my number and placed it in her hand, closing her hand shut around the paper and walking away.

She stood on the sidewalk, looking at me, as I walked away until I was out of view. It's sad, another woman fell victim to Norris. I couldn't help but wonder if Allie knew he had a STD. It wasn't too long ago him and his girl had that shit going on. It wasn't my place to speak on it, so I didn't. I felt sorry for her; but then again, I didn't.

Chapter 9

"No Strings Attached"

The day I'd been dreading, but waiting for at the same time, was finally here. We were going to court to finalize the divorce and settle our assets. I was represented by my lawyer and Chris had one too. When he saw me, he stared, as usual. He came alone, this time. Chanel was nowhere to be found. Maybe it was because he had that bitch pregnant and didn't know I knew. Maybe that's why she was hiding all along. I hadn't spoken to him since I called him after him and Daddy got into it.

I had no intentions on being greedy in court. I just wanted what I deserved. I was a boss bitch not a bum bitch. I didn't want anything to do with his club, his personal belongings or his money. I had my own. I just wanted everything to be fair. The houses were in our names, so I wanted to sell it and split the profit for both.

Him and Chanel were still living in the Atlanta home, which I gave no fucks about. They would have to find someplace else to lay their heads. They were lucky I wasn't a bitch, putting them out of a home when they least expected it. When I wanted to sell the home in Charlotte and had buyers, Chris backed out at the last minute. I shouldn't be as lenient with him as I am because he doesn't deserve it.

When the judge asked my wishes, my lawyer politely told her that all I wanted was a finalized divorce and to sell both homes and split the money. I didn't want anything else. But when the judge asked for Chris' wishes, it was a totally different story. This man was outrageous with the things he asked for.

He wanted to sell the Charlotte home and split the profit on that. He wanted to remain in the Atlanta home with his baby mama he failed to mention, and he wanted to own half of my boutique and wanted half of what I had in my account. He was out of his damn mind. He built his shit on his own and I did the same. Even when we were together, he paid for nothing that involved my boutique. I still had money sitting in the bank from my parents' death. That had nothing to do with him either. He wanted shit he wasn't entitled to.

I knew he wouldn't make it easy. He came in with a game plan, not knowing he would lose. There were so many things I could have said, but I kept it cool. He gave Chanel the $20,000 to pay me, just to try and get it back in court. He wanted to stay in the Atlanta home because he hadn't been looking for anywhere else to go.

I knew he would come back for revenge. He wanted to make it work with me and I declined his offer. He was jealous that I had moved on. He was upset that I wasn't showing him that I cared about him or giving him any attention. He wanted to destroy me and everything that I built because I didn't take him back.

I prayed that the judge saw it was all bullshit and that he didn't deserve what he asked for. Sure enough, the judge did. My prayers were answered. Once again, my worries were lifted. I could breathe again.

I got exactly what I asked for. The judge told Chris that he was a fool and out of his mind for asking for the things that he did. She saw him as I saw him. Once again, with a good team on my side, we won, for the second time.

I was finally free from him. Now, I could live my life with Daddy without feeling guilty for breaking the vows I should have never made in the first place. Daddy and I were celebrating by going out for dinner and drinks for about a week. I didn't have any thoughts or concerns about Chris. I didn't call or text him once, after leaving that courtroom, but he didn't waste much time reaching out to me.

He called me, begging me to let him stay in the house because he had nowhere to go. He apologized to me for trying to take my money and my business. I didn't care about him not having a place to go because if he hadn't done the things he did, he would have had a home. I was still upset about him trying to take my money and half of my business too.

Damn, just a few months ago, I was stressed out. I didn't know where life would take me or if it was even worth living because of the situations I was in with fake friends and disloyal family. Now, they were stressed out, reaching out to me for help, stressing like I did when they didn't give a fuck about me. Now, I was sitting back watching karma kick their asses.

I was in a better place! Stress free with no worries... Working on my happiness... Finally, living with joy. No drama! I was receiving the love I always deserved. It felt good. The tables turned so quickly. What they were dealing with was so much better than seeking revenge.

I don't know what woman in their right mind would believe that his apology was sincere, but I wasn't that chick to believe him. I went through with the process of selling both homes. Two months later, I got a call from my attorney and was filled with joy. I was getting closer and closer to being done with Chris completely. My life was coming together, again.

As time went by, I thought heavily about what I should do with all of this money. I was still indecisive about getting a second location for the boutique. I didn't know if I wanted to buy a house out-of-town, or even if I wanted to buy a house with Chris at all. Gracie was always my go-to when I needed to vent or seek advice. I was just about to hit her up, when she buzzed my line.

"Hey, girl!" Gracie said.

"What's up? I was just about to call you."

"I'll never forgive you for the request to sell both of y'all's houses!"

Laughing, I said, "Why not? What's wrong?"

"Because Chris and his girl are here!"

"What? No way! How did they end up there, out of all places they could've went?"

"Girl! Chris asked Josh if they could stay until they found a place. You knew me and her don't really talk, so it's awkward, but I'm managing. The second she disrespects me, she's out!"

"Wow! With all that money he has, he couldn't get a quick spot for them? Even if it's an apartment, something would do."

"I don't know what they have going on, but they can't stay here longer than a month."

"Kick their asses out! I don't blame you!"

"I don't mean to be mean, but we need our space. A month is more than enough time to find a place."

"Exactly!"

When Daddy was around, I always tried not to mention or talk about Chris or Norris, as I knew how much it bothered him.

"Anthony just walked in; let me call you back in a bit."

I always felt guilty about leaving my girl hanging when my man came around, even though she did the same to me. When Daddy came in, he asked me if I wanted to go house hunting. Ever since he sold his place, he had been talking about buying a house a lot, but I never really told him my true feelings about it.

"Are you sure it's the right time?" I asked him.

"Baby, yes! I've already spoken to a realtor. She'll be meeting us at the place in a few hours."

Since he already had things planned, I couldn't leave him hanging. So, I got up and headed out the door to look at a few houses the realtor was showing.

All day we'd been searching and still found nothing, which I took as a sign. Something just didn't seem right. The entire time we looked at houses, I thought about how I could tell him that I wasn't ready.

"Daddy?"

"Yes, my love?"

"Why don't we hold off on buying a house. What's the rush about it anyway?"

"I want to make you happy."

"That time will come when it's supposed to. These are nice and all - I lied - but I haven't found the one. I want what I want. These are not what I want, so let's just wait," I told him.

"Baby, I want you to be-"

"Daddy, let's just wait. How about we focus on us making more money, you getting your own law firm and me expanding and getting another location?" I batted my eyes and gave him a puppy dog look, hoping he would agree with me.

"Baby?"

"Please," I continued to beg.

"Ok," he replied.

The realtor stood behind us, as we talked, and then I realized we were never introduced to each other.

"I'm sorry, Anthony is rude. I'm Tara, his girlfriend," I said to her, as I went in to shake her hand.

"Hi, I'm Asia. Nice to finally meet you, Tara."

"I'm sorry, ladies, my bad," Daddy chimed in.

"Oh, no worries, I got this," I replied to Anthony.

Daddy walked off and started wandering around the house.

"Do you guys know each other?" I asked.

"Actually, we do," Asia said, with a smirk.

"Oh, ok. I didn't know that. So, how long have y'all known each other?" I asked.

Asia looked around, blushing, before replying, "Anthony and I grew up together. We've known each other all our lives. He calls me to help him when he's looking to buy or sell a house. We have history."

"Oh, history?"

"Yeah," Asia replied.

Daddy came back, stood next to me and asked if I was ready to go.

I took a good look at Asia and told her, "It's been nice chatting with you."

"It was a pleasure meeting you, Tara. I'm sure I'll be seeing more of you."

"Yes, the hell… yes, yes you will!" I replied.

We went to part ways, but before we walked off, Asia smirked, touched Daddy on the shoulder and said, "Call me if you need me."

Daddy and I got in the car and I pouted the entire ride home, not speaking to him or looking in his direction. Something wasn't right with him and Asia. When we got to the house, I went straight to the bedroom.

"Baby?"

"Tara?" Daddy continued.

"Don't fuckin' talk to me, unless you want to tell me what the fuck was up with that Asia bitch!"

"Nothing's up with her. What do you mean?"

"Nigga, I'm not dumb!"

"I know you're not, baby! I never said you was."

"Well, tell me! She's definitely more than you're fuckin' realtor!"

"Yes, she is. She's a childhood friend."

"Well, why hadn't I met her before today?"

"I don't know, baby. I'm sorry! It's not that serious. I would never fuck with Asia, baby! We're too close. She's like a homegirl."

"I got my eyes on that bitch...and you too. Let that bitch know that friendly shit ain't gon' cut it and I won't hesitate to beat her ass!"

Daddy laughed, as if I wasn't serious. He came over to me, as I sat on the bed, stood between my legs, grabbed my face, and kissed my forehead.

"Calm down, baby. This dick is yours. You know that!"

I rolled my eyes and said, "Yeah, I know, Daddy!"

"You be trippin' for no reason sometimes."

"I love you, Daddy..."

"I love you too, baby."

Chapter 10

"How Does It Feel?"

With so much on my mind, I decided to go over to Gracie's. Chris and his bitch weren't there, so it was perfect. I had no desire to see those fools.

Gracie was getting fed up with their arguing and how disrespectful Chanel had been to her. She needed to vent and so did I. When she called me over for some gossip and wine, there was no way in hell I could turn it down.

"Girl," Gracie said to me, after downing her glass of wine.

"Let it out! I know how it is, bitch! You don't have to sugarcoat shit with a real friend who knows all about these motherfuckers," I told her.

"I don't know where to begin."

"From the beginning," I told her, as I poured her more wine.

"I don't know why we allowed them to stay here, but they have to go ASAP! First of all, they argue almost every night! They wake us up all times of the night, Chanel doesn't speak much, and she walks around here like we owe her something. Josh and I haven't said much to her, to keep the peace, but I can't take much more of this, Tara."

"What made them come here in the first place? She never liked your bougie-ass anyway. Remember, she would always call you a bougie bitch?" I reminded her.

We laughed, and Gracie said, "You know what, Tara, you're right! I forgot about that big blowup she caused between us at dinner."

"Well, if you don't want them here, sis, put their asses out. This is your place! You are not obligated to take care of grown-ass people anyway. They can go somewhere else. Chris has money. He needs to put them in something - even if it's not nice. How the fuck can you give a bitch you haven't been with for a year $20,000, but can't pay for a place to stay? That club is always busy! They make money; he got it! He's just being a cheap bitch! Don't let them fool y'all."

"You're right, but I will feel terrible putting them out with no place to stay. I don't want to cause tension between Josh and I."

"Listen! Josh probably wants their asses out just as much as you do!"

"Oh yeah, he has been trippin' lately because I haven't been giving him no pussy since they've been here. I told him I'm not fuckin' him while they're here. Hell no!"

"No nigga likes waiting for pussy, so do what you have to do."

When we were done talking, we drank the last bit of wine we had. Gracie poured more in our glasses and we heard keys at the door. When we turned around, Chanel and Chris walked in.

I started smackin' my lips and muggin' them both, as they walked through the door. Keeping my composure was difficult, and there was no way in hell I was gonna try when I didn't give a fuck about either of them.

Gracie looked at me, and I looked back at her. She looked at Chanel and Chris and they stared back. The moment was awkward as hell. When they went upstairs, Gracie looked at me and said, "It's showtime."

I looked at her and said, "Do what you gotta do, boo, just know I got yo' back."

They portrayed their lives and relationship to be so perfect, when it was far from it. They couldn't fool me. I knew the both of them like the back of my hands. I knew from the start what it would be.

Gracie got up and stood at the bottom of the stairs, yelling, "Chris…Chanel, can y'all come down for a minute?"

They didn't respond, so she yelled it again.

"Be down in a minute… damn," Chanel hollered.

Gracie stood at the bottom of the stairs for a minute longer. She looked at me, in shock, walked over to the sofa I sat on and said, "I've had enough of her and her attitude. She has to go! Did you just hear that?"

"Oh, I did! You can't help ungrateful bitches! I learned that a long time ago," I said, shaking my head.

Gracie shook her head and sipped some more wine.

"Hey. What's up," Chris asked Gracie.

Chanel just stood beside Chris with her arms crossed.

Gracie started the conversation.

"Listen, I've been trying to be patient with y'all finding a place, but it's not working out. The bickering back and forth, waking us up at night, Chanel's being disrespectful to me, and I feel like my kindness is being takin' for granted. I need y'all out by tomorrow evening."

"It's cool, Gracie. I apologize for all of that and I understand completely. We will be gone by tomorrow."

"Thanks, Chris."

"How the fuck you mean it's cool? We don't have any place else to go! That's why we were here in the first place," Chanel argued.

"Shut the fuck up, for once, Chanel. Damn! You really pissin' me off," Chris yelled.

Chris started walking off and Chanel grabbed him by the shirt. He turned around with one fist balled up, grabbed her face with the other hand and held it. He stared at her with the same look he gave me before he whipped my ass.

Gracie hopped up off the couch and ran over to them.

"Stop it, Chris," Gracie hollered, but he didn't listen.

She said it again, but louder. I saw him snap back into reality and look over to Gracie, still squeezing Chanel's face. I sat my happily-peaceful-ass right on the sofa. Gracie went over to save that ho, but I, on the other hand, was gonna let him beat her ass like he used to do me. She begged for him. Now, she got what she asked for.

Chanel and Chris went upstairs, and Gracie came back over to me.

"I can't take this, Tara; this is what I was talking about. Chris is crazy! I can't have that in my house. If she doesn't leave him alone, he will end up killing her."

"Listen, girl, you ain't tellin' me nothin' I don't already know. I've been there and dealt with that. Chris acts innocent around people who don't truly know him, but really, he is the fuckin' devil! When he was about to beat the shit out of her a second ago, I sat my ass right here. You wanna know why? Because she wanted that! She begged for him! She went behind my back, and slept with my husband. So, hell no, I'm not saving her. Whatever drama they have is beyond me."

I continued, "I'm so damn happy, Gracie! I'm happy with my life! I'm happy with my man! I'm happy Chris and I are officially done! I'm happy none of those fake bitches are around me anymore. When I see Chanel and Chris, I see myself and him. The old Tara. She will have to learn on her own."

"I know your mad with her still, but-"

"No, Gracie, let me stop you right there. I'm done with them both. I'm not mad at all. I used to be, but not anymore."

"Well, I can't sit here and watch him beat her!"

"You go on and get in it if you want to, but I won't! When I was getting my ass beat by him, was she there? When I told her what I was going through with him, was she helpful? Fuck her!"

"I get it, Tara. Let's just kill this conversation before it gets out of hand. They will be leaving soon; we will have our place back to ourselves and there will be no more drama."

"Cheers to that!" I said.

We both laughed and turned the TV on. We tuned into Love and Hip-Hop Atlanta, trying to catch up, since we missed the last few episodes. Halfway through the episode, I heard noise coming from upstairs.

"Gracie, you hear that?"

"No! Hear what?"

"Pause the TV."

"Listen," I told her.

We sat on the couch and we heard arguing and noise like something was hitting the wall.

Gracie hopped up, once again, and ran upstairs. This time, I went right behind her.

As we ran up the stairs, we heard yelling and screaming. Gracie banged on the bedroom door and yelled, "Open up this door! Open this door." No one came to open the door, so she continued to bang and yell. They still didn't open the door, so we knocked it down. When we opened the door, what I saw gave me a flashback.

Entering the room, Chris had his hand around Chanel's neck. Chanel looked over to us with tears in her eyes.

"Let her go! Just let her go, Chris," I yelled.

He yelled back at us, "This don't have shit to do with y'all! Mind your fuckin' business!"

Gracie threatened to call the cops, and then Chris turned Chanel's neck loose. Chanel looked over to us, with tears covering her face, holding her neck, and whispered thank you.

Chris started grabbing all of his bags. Before he walked out the room, he turned around, looked at Chanel and said, "Fuck you! I'm leaving your stupid-ass!"

Chanel jumped up, pushing us out the way to run behind Chris. She hollered at him, as he went down the stairs. "Where are you going? Chris, come back!"

"I'm going to Atlanta - where I belong."

"So, you have some place to stay?" Chanel asked, in shock.

"Yes, and you're not invited."

Chanel started crying.

"Where am I supposed to go?"

"Wherever the hell you want! You are not my concern anymore."

"I may not be, but the baby should. So, you're going to leave the mother of your child homeless and helpless? Is that what you're telling me?"

"We'll figure something out for the baby, when the time comes."

"Well, can you at least leave me some money, until I figure things out?"

"I'm leaving you the car and $500," Chris continued.

"What the hell am I supposed to do with $500, Chris? That ain't enough!"

"If your ass had a job, you wouldn't be in this predicament, now would you?"

"But we agreed to this," Chanel cried.

"And that's where I fucked up at," Chris hollered, before slamming the car door behind him.

Chapter 11

"A Hurting Mother"

I was lying in the bed, scrolling on Facebook, as I waited for Daddy to finish breakfast. Chanel and I were still friends on it, and she was on my mind heavily, since I witnessed the fight her and Chris had. She was on Facebook Live, so I joined to watch. "When you got a fuck nigga as a baby daddy, but your brother always come through for you," Chanel said, right before hitting the blunt. "Yeah, nigga, you are a bitch! I will see you when I see you," Norris chimed in.

Who was the bitch on my phone right now? She was being ratchet and reckless… Smoking weed while she was pregnant, putting the world in her business, and getting into some serious shit with the threats she was making. From all the noise on my phone, Daddy came running in the room.

"What the hell is that, baby? What you got going on?"

"I was watching Chanel's Live. Just bullshit and drama, as usual," I said.

"Do you remember when I told you what happened at Gracie's?"

"Yeah," Daddy replied.

"Well, apparently, her and everybody else is beefing with Chris now, after all of that."

"Well, that's what she gets! It ain't too much I can say about that because she caused that on herself," Daddy said.

"I felt the same way, until I witnessed how he treated her."

"So, are you wanting to settle things between y'all? I don't think it's a good idea."

"I don't know. Let me just say I don't hate the bitch at all! I'm just disappointed in her and hate that she would do such a thing to one of the few people that held her down. I really miss her, though. I really do!" I told Daddy.

I didn't hold Daddy up with talking about Chanel's nonsense too long. He had to get to work, so I wanted to enjoy my man while I could and not waste our time talking about irrelevant shit. We only had an hour together, before it was time for him to head out. After we ate breakfast, he got ready and left.

It was just Mani and I at the house; and although I was just waking up, I was still exhausted. I was overdue for a break, so I could get some sleep, prop my feet up and relax. I reached out to our sitter, only to find out that she was on vacation.

Daddy had plans on being at work late, so waiting on him would be pointless. Gracie and Josh weren't available either. I was out of luck. So I thought. Until I realized I had a whole baby daddy. I knew I said I would not talk to him or be around him, but I was desperate as hell for a break, so I hit him up.

Norris picked up the phone.

"Norris, what are you doing?"

"Shit. I'm just chilling… What's up?"

"Any plans for today?" I asked.

"No! What's up?"

"Can you come over to the house to watch Mani, while I get some sleep?"

"Yeah, what time?"

"Now is good..." I told him.

"Alright, I'm on the way."

"I'll text you the address. Don't share my shit and don't bring anybody else here!"

"Chill, man. Why would I do some shit like that? Why are you always all hostile and shit with me?"

"Just hurry up and get here," I told him.

Norris came by alone. I was able to clean up, start washing and drying clothes in peace and take a two-hour nap. When I woke up, Norris and Mani were gone. I ran around the house, trying to find my phone. My hands were shaking, as I called him. I paced back and forth in the living room, waiting for him to pick up.

"Please, pick up," I whispered, repeatedly, over and over to myself. I called him twice and got no answer. I got so annoyed with him not answering, so I hung up the phone and threw it across the room.

"That's why I don't ask this nigga to do shit! He is fuckin' stupid. I never told him to take my child out of this house! Why did he take her out the house?" I hollered, as I hit on the door repeatedly.

I sat down on the couch, with my hands on my head. I thought about what could be going on and where they could be. I tried not to think the worst because I was trying to stay calm.

After I calmed down, I went to pick up my phone off the floor and called him again, but of course, there was still no answer.

I didn't have Chanel's number. Michelle had been calling me from a blocked number lately, and the number I did have for her was disconnected. I called Josh, but he didn't pick up either. I called Gracie, but it went straight to voicemail. I sat back down on the couch and thought about whether I should stay home just in case they came back, or if I should go over to his place to see if they were there.

I got angrier waiting on him, so I snatched my keys off the counter, hopped in my whip and sped the entire way to Norris' place. I didn't see his car in the parking lot when I pulled up, but I still went to his door. I banged on the door. *Boom, boom, boom, boom!* Nobody came, so I banged some more. I was so loud, one of his neighbors stuck her head out of her door, trying to see what all the noise was about.

The little, old lady asked, "Is everything ok, sweetie?"

"Yes, ma'am."

"Have you seen the guy that lives here at all today, by chance?" I asked her.

"Well, I only saw him around noon when he was leaving out. Are you sure everything is ok? He is such a sweet, respectful young man. He speaks to me all the time."

"Everything is fine! If you see him, can you tell him Tara was by?"

"Sure thing, Tara."

Nobody answered the door, so I left. I sat in the car in front of his apartment for about thirty minutes, talking shit, crying and beating on my car door. The sun was starting to set, and I hadn't seen my daughter for hours.

I couldn't get in touch with Norris and I was worried sick about my child. When I pulled off to head to the police station, my phone rang. It wasn't Norris, but it was Gracie.

"Girl, I've been trying to call you all day. I-"

"Tara, stop! Have you heard?" She asked.

"Heard what?" I asked, in a frightened voice. When Gracie said that, I felt it in my gut that something was wrong.

"Norris was shot! He's at the hospital!"

"When, Gracie?"

"A few hours ago, to be exact!"

"A few hours ago? Where is my damn child? I've been trying to find her all day."

"What do you mean find her?" Gracie asked.

"Norris came over to watch her while I got some things done at the house and caught up on some sleep. I took a nap, woke up and they were gone. I haven't heard from him since. Where the fuck is my child, Gracie?"

"Calm down, Tara. Where are you?"

"Leaving Norris' place to head to the police station. I need to go to whichever hospital he is at, so I can find out where my child is!"

"He's at the Carolinas Medical Center. I'll meet you there," Gracie said.

When Gracie told me that, I rushed to get to the hospital, hoping and praying the whole ride there that my child was ok. I didn't want to have to flip out on Norris while he was going through all of this; but if I had to, I would. I was hoping that she was good, though, so I can keep my cool. I was so damn pissed at him, I couldn't promise anyone, not even myself, that I would.

I thought about how I went back on my word and gave this fool the benefit of the doubt. I was still upset with him and didn't want anything to do with him with all the shit he had going on. I was chill, when he came. I didn't talk to him nastily and I tried not to be argumentative - even though there was so much shit I could argue with him about - and this is what happens. I knew I couldn't trust him. I wish I never called him. If my child wasn't ok when I got there, all hell would break loose.

I sped to the hospital, with no thoughts of getting in an accident or pulled over by the police. I was ready to get to my girl, and make sure she was ok. Gracie never told me what room Norris was in, so I walked up to the help desk.

"Hi! I'm trying to find which room Norris Montgomery is in.

"Ok, let me just take a look here and see what I can help you with," the receptionist said.

"Thank you so much," I replied.

I waited patiently for the receptionist to tell me which room he was in, hoping that I would be one step closer to finding my child.

"Ma'am, I'm sorry, but I cannot disclose that information," the receptionist said.

I frowned and said, "Listen, lady, my baby daddy was shot, he had my kid with him. I need to go find out where my child is so I can get her. I don't give a fuck about him and what he has going on. Can you help me figure out where my child is, then?"

"Ma'am, if your child is missing, then you will need to call the cops. I'm a receptionist."

"I didn't ask you what the fuck you are! Clearly, you're a receptionist, and a pathetic one at that! There has to be some sort of protocol for situations like this," I hollered.

"I'm sorry, ma'am, but unfortunately there's nothing I can do!"

"Fuck you, lady, you're not even trying."

I walked off and was headed out the front door to call Gracie, when I saw her walking in, and I heard Josh's voice behind me. I knew God would make a way for me. He always had.

They took me up the stairs to the waiting area where everyone was. When I got to the waiting area, I saw my baby. I wasn't pleased at all that Chanel had her, but when she handed her over to me, I felt that same feeling I felt when I delivered her and saw her for the first time. I didn't argue with Chanel this time, I was grateful that she was ok.

I noticed there was a guy sitting in the corner away from everybody else. The guy looked like Anthony's brother. I remembered seeing him in a picture Daddy showed me of all of them the night he came back from chilling with them.

Why was he here, though, looking suspicious as hell in the corner? Then, what Daddy told me came to me. "Oh shit," I whispered. I stood there, staring at him, with so many thoughts running through my head. When I saw him getting up, I turned my head quickly in the opposite direction. He walked up to me and whispered in my ear.

"I hope this nigga is dead. If he ain't, he will be. I know who you are and if I find out that you repeated this, you and this little, precious baby will be too."

I stood, speechless, staring off into space, trying to take in everything that was said to me. I made no movement, there was no talking, or blinking. Shortly after he left from by me, Gracie walked over to me and asked, "Are you ok, girl?"

I didn't respond. I was too focused on making sure Anthony's brother was leaving. While he completely parted ways from us, he looked back at me - one final time - and winked his eye. I waited a few minutes, in fear, before sitting; just to make sure he was really gone.

It was me, Josh, Gracie, Steven, Chanel, Rocko and Michelle in the waiting area, until Allie walked up. She was starting to show more, since the last time I'd seen and spoken to her. She came over and hugged me.

"Good to see you again," she said to me.

When I looked over at Michelle, I saw her give Allie the side-eye. I assumed they hadn't made up from their last altercation, by the way she looked at her. I concluded that Michelle didn't know she would show up either. Allie greeted everyone, and everyone greeted her back, except Michelle.

"Hey, Chelle," Allie said, singling her out, but Michelle still didn't speak.

"Well, y'all, I don't know what the fuck her problem is, but clearly she is mad about something," Allie said, as she sat down laughing.

"Do I fuck with you, though? Answer that!" Michelle replied.

"Girl, bye, I could care less if you fuck with me or not. I know who do, though," Allie said, with a smirk on her face.

As we sat in the waiting area, it felt like déjà vu. Just a few years ago, we sat in the same waiting area praying for this nigga... Hoping this idiot was ok. This time, it was totally different. The room was filled with drama and people with senseless beef with one another. No one knew Norris would have us sitting here, once again.

When it was time to go in the back with Norris, we all formed a line, as we went in the room. Norris was up, talking to the few people that were ahead of me. As soon as I walked through the door with Mani in my arms, his heart rate gradually went higher.

"I'm sorry, Tara. I didn't know..." Norris tried explaining.

"Listen, it's been a long day and I don't even want to hear it right now. I'm so pissed, it's best I keep my conversation with you short. I just came to see how you was and let her see her daddy before we left. Best believe, this bullshit you pulled today will be the last time because you won't be seeing her for a while," I hollered past Allie, who stood in front of me.

Michelle was first in line and ran up to Norris and started kissing him on the forehead, rubbing on his face, but I could see him moving away from her. He kept glancing over to Allie, as she waited in line behind Chanel.

"Man, Brother, you have to be more careful. This has been the second scare. I've already lost Mama, I can't lose you too."

"I know, sis. I'm trying to make a change. I really am!"

"Leave the streets alone, bro. It ain't worth it."

"I am serious. I can't do this. Being shot is painful, having to keep coming to the hospital, not knowing if I'm going to leave is a hurtful feeling too. My daughter was with me. That really fucked me up. Y'all really think I would put her in the middle of something like this on purpose? All because of these niggas, I can't see my fuckin' daughter. I love my daughter, brah… I love my fuckin' daughter. Thankfully, it's me lying here and not her," Norris cried.

"This shit ain't my fault," Norris continued.

Allie stood in front of me in the line. When she went up to him, she kissed him on the cheek.

"Norris, please don't scare me like this again. I thought you were dead. I need you here… we need you here," Allie said to him.

Norris looked down at her stomach, looked over to Michelle, Michelle looked at them both and I looked at all of them. I hoped to tell him our goodbyes before all hell broke loose, but it was too late.

Michelle got up and walked over to them. I kid you not, every time I was in a hospital room with one of Ms. Sherlene's kids, some crazy shit happened.

"Who the fuck is we?" Michelle asked.

Chanel got up and went by them. "Not in here, ok? Y'all just chill the fuck out!" Chanel hollered.

"I'm assuming you didn't tell her," Allie said to Norris.

"What is going on?" Michelle asked him.

"I'm pregnant by yo' nigga!" Allie bragged.

Chapter 12

"The Fuck Up"

"**G**et up, bitch! I warned you, but you didn't listen! Until I get Norris, you will never see your baby! If I don't get him in 24 hours, starting now, you both are dead," I heard Anthony's brother's voice.

Tossing and turning in my sleep, I got a tap on my shoulder. I hopped up out my sleep, terrified, looking around the room, as if it was filled with heavyset black men strapped with guns. I found Daddy sitting next to me, and I realized it was only a nightmare.

"Baby, what's wrong? I've watched you for the past hour and a half. Something is going on, so tell me what's wrong."

"Where's my baby?" I asked, jumping out the bed, paranoid as hell.

I ran in her room, grabbed her out the bed and held her in my arms, kissing on her repeatedly. Tears filled my eyes. Daddy walked in the room and asked me, again, "What's going on, baby?"

"Nothing! I'm fine," I told him.

"You're not!"

"Listen, I got some shit going on that I just can't talk about," I explained.

He grabbed Mani out my arms, placed her back in bed and grabbed me by the hand, dragging me to the dining room and sitting me down at the table.

He got on his knees, between my legs, and held my hands tightly. He looked me in my eyes and said, "Baby! There is no way that I am going to believe everything is fine. The entire time we have been together, I have never seen you like this. You have gone through some shit, but you have never done anything like this. It's 2am and you haven't slept for the past few days. I know something is wrong. I can't help you unless you talk to me. Now, tell me! What's wrong?"

I snatched my hands away from him. I turned my entire body and put my hands on my head, crying heavily. Something in me told me to keep it to myself, but Daddy said he could help. I knew I shouldn't have said anything, but I told him anyway. So, no, I couldn't keep my big-ass mouth shut.

I told him what happened from the time I called Norris over to watch baby girl, to what his brother said to me in the waiting area at the hospital. Daddy got up and walked in the kitchen. He leaned over the counter, with his hands on his head. I watched him twist up his mouth and the veins pop on his forehead. He banged on the counter, infuriated.

"Damn! I told you to stay away from him!"

"Listen, I tried. How long do you expect me to stay away from him when he's my child's father? We share a baby together, and sometimes I need him to step in and help me. It's not that easy to just walk away. You don't have kids, so you don't understand."

"Now look what you got us into," Daddy said.

"I thought you said you could help. That's the only reason why I told you. I don't need to hear this shit right now; I'm stressed enough already. I wouldn't have told you, if I knew this would happen."

Daddy walked over to me, got down on his knees between my legs, again, and grabbed me by the waist, pulling me closer to him.

"I got you, baby. I'm sorry. I'm just mad! Mad that y'all are caught up in all of this now! I will try and protect y'all."

"What do you mean try?" I asked.

"I will do all that I can, ok?" He replied.

I was relieved, once I heard Daddy say that, knowing he would still be here to protect us, even if he had to go up against his own blood. I went back to bed, and tried to ease my mind about the nightmare and get some sleep before morning.

I laid in bed, thinking about what Anthony's brother whispered in my ear. I thought about all the trouble Norris had brought in my life and realized it was his fault - once again. I said, many times, that I was happy to not be with him or have to deal with his shit; but truth was, he was still putting me through hell, even though we weren't together. I contemplated what needed to change and how I could get my family out of this.

When I woke up, I realized, after talking to Daddy, I slept and felt a little better. I was holding him to what he told me about protecting us. I knew that was his family, so if he ever went back on his word, we would be screwed.

I hadn't spoken to Norris since I left the hospital. I heard from Gracie that he should be going home soon, if he wasn't home already. I was dying to talk to him about why he took Mani while I was asleep and express to him my frustration about his decision. Not like it would change his way of thinking, or even change what already happened, but he needed to hear me out and understand the severity. My child could have been dead. I never had the chance to get details about what happened. Since Daddy was out for a few hours, I decided to call him - for the last and final time.

"Yo'," Norris answered.

"Do you have time to talk?" I asked.

"Yeah, what's up?"

"How are you feelin'?"

"Still in some pain, but I'll be good, he replied"

"So, do you know who did this to you?"

"I think yo' bitch-ass husband had something to do with it."

"Correction, ex-husband, but why do you think that?"

"We've been beefin' since he played my sister. Man, listen, you askin' too many questions. They did me dirty while I had baby girl in the car with me, and just know I'm not gonna let that slide. They will get dealt with. This situation will be handled; it won't happen again," he said.

"Yeah, I know it won't. I was worried about where my child was, and then I got a phone call that she was practically about to lose her life for some shit you got her into…us into. It's not safe. You have all this going on; meanwhile, I'm over here stressing and concerned about our safety."

"Tara, listen! I got this. We will be good."

"You always say that, Norris. Whoever did this tried to kill you. They don't give a fuck about you, and will do whatever they need to see you dead... Even if that involves hurting us," I told him.

"Man..."

"I called to check on you and to let you know that I don't want anything to do with you. I don't want you to call me, come by or anything. For the sake of our safety, I will take care of Mani by myself - like I did before. When you get your life together, then maybe, just maybe, we can work some things out. Until then, don't bother us," I told Norris, just before ending our call.

Norris called back as soon as I hung up, but I didn't answer. I put him back on the block list. This shit wasn't a game. They were really out to get him. I heard them say it myself. My dream was confirmation that I needed to make some moves before it was too late, and I did just that.

I got up and gathered myself because Gracie and her baby girl were coming over to the house to visit. She'd been worried about me, 'since I was actin' strange in the hospital,' as she called it. I never mentioned what really bothered me. I kept it short... "Norris has been stressin' me the hell out."

When she got there, we started chatting and drinking our wine, catching up on how each other's lives were since our last sit-down at her house when Chris and Chanel had drama. Talking about them lead me to ask her if she heard from any of them lately.

She told me that she kept in contact with Chanel after she saved her at the house, and that Chanel told her that her and Chris were really done with each other. Gracie said he never turned back, after leaving her the day he walked out on her. She told me Chanel was living with Norris and Michelle, she was still pregnant, but Gracie didn't know how far along she was.

"How the hell are they going to raise a baby and they can't get along now?" I inquired.

"Girl, your guess is just as good as mine. It's gon' be hell for her."

"That's what she wanted, girl," I said, as I sipped my wine.

"Do you think y'all will ever be able to be cool again, now that her and Chris is done?"

"Anthony asked me the same thing, and quite frankly, I really can't say. Just because they're done doesn't mean she can come running back to me now. She burnt bridges that can't be rebuilt, unless it's from scratch… and even if it is, it will never be the same as before. That doesn't undo the shit she has already done, and it would be so awkward. Especially, since she's pregnant with my ex-husband's baby. I was once mad that he gave her the baby I was supposed to have, but now that I look back at things, I'm glad Mani isn't his."

"Really? So, you would prefer to deal with Norris than Chris?"

"Yes, girl."

"Why though?" Gracie asked.

"Honestly, Chris is an asshole. The only thing he is good at is spending money, surprises and fucking. I don't regret our relationship, nor our marriage because it wasn't all bad. We did have some fun times together, but…"

"But…?" Gracie asked.

"He has anger issues. Really bad! I couldn't deal with him abusing me. I know for sure if I had a kid by him, and we broke up, he would still abuse me if he didn't have his way. Being with him is not worth dealing with that. He was antagonizing, many times; especially, after he got drunk. Norris' problems are lying, cheating and commitment. Now that we aren't together, that doesn't even matter anymore. He does his part and I do mine."

"Have you talked to him?"

I rolled my eyes and said, "Yeah…"

"Girl, I can already tell y'all had an argument," Gracie said, shaking her head.

"No, not really. I told him straight up, I'm concerned about our safety and not to contact me about anything until he gets his shit together. And, of course, he took what happened to him lightly, as if it wasn't a big deal. 'Uh… listen, Tara, I got it all under control, don't worry. Y'all are good.' Blah, blah. He thinks it's a game, girl."

"So, what about him helping you with Mani?"

"I don't give a damn about him helping. Ain't like I haven't done this shit by myself before. Anthony is a great father figure to her. She will be good, Gracie. I hate that I have to keep her away from him when they were just getting to know each other, but it's for everybody's best interest - especially, hers."

"I could have lost her that night, Gracie. To some bullshit she had absolutely nothin' to do with. I still think about that every day and I will never forget it."

"Yeah, you're right. I understand, though. We have to protect these kids by all means. Even if we have to do things we will probably regret later," Gracie replied.

"And that's exactly what I'm going to do," I told her.

"Tara, can you watch Gracelyn for a second? I need to take this call," Gracie said, before walking towards the front door.

"Sure, girl, go ahead."

I sat on the floor and started playing with the girls, while Gracie went to take her call. It was fun having them together and getting to see how they interacted with one another. I smiled, constantly, as I watched them. I wanted a kid with Anthony, but we never talked about it. I could get used to having two babies in the house.

Gracie came back over five minutes later and asked if I wanted to ride with her. I didn't have shit to do and I could use a getaway from the house to take my mind off things, so I went to put on some decent clothes, and we headed out. Daddy didn't know I was leaving the house today, so I sent him a quick text, letting him know I was with Gracie, just so he didn't have to worry.

The entire ride, I looked out the window, wondering where Gracie was taking me because she refused to tell me anything. We headed Downtown and came up on the hospital. The same hospital Norris was at.

"What the hell are we doing here, Gracie? I just told you I was trying to stay away from this nigga. I ain't trying to see him!"

"Norris isn't here. He's home."

"So, what the hell are we doing here?" I repeated.

"It's Chanel. She called me and asked me to come over."

"And that's even worse. She asked *you* to come. What does that have to do with me?"

"Tara, don't be like that. You know you miss her. I know you miss her. This would be a nice time for y'all to make up."

I rolled my eyes at Gracie. She always played the peacemaker. As I sat there in the car, while Gracie looked for a parking spot, I realized going in wouldn't be a bad idea after all. I didn't know what was going on but I damn sure wanted to find out. I was going to take my nosy-ass right in that hospital. I planned to act caring and sympathetic to her.

Chapter 13

"Secret Lover"

Ｗe walked in the hospital and came up on the help desk. I stood there, again, looking for help. It left us no choice but to deal with that nasty, rude-ass receptionist that I dealt with when I was coming to check on Norris. This time, there was another lady at the desk, standing beside her. The lady beside her was a supervisor, as it said on her name tag.

The rude receptionist was in a great mood - this time. She even stood and acknowledged us when we approached the desk.

"Hi. I'm looking for Ch-" Gracie started to tell her, but then I nudged her in the side. When she looked at me, I winked.

"Hi. We are looking to find out which room Chanel Montgomery is in. Would you ladies be able to help us with that?" I asked, smiling at the rude-ass receptionist.

She paused and looked deeply in my eyes, realizing that I was the one she had been a bitch to the other day. Finally, she spoke, after snapping back to reality and realizing her supervisor stood less than a half foot away from her.

"Sure," she replied.

The supervisor looked at us with a big, beautiful smile and said, "We will get you ladies taken care of."

"Thank you so much," I said to her. The rude receptionist looked up at me, periodically. She must have felt that I was up to no good. I wasn't leaving the desk without being the bitch that she was to me.

"May I have your ID's," the rude receptionist asked.

"Sure, I told her." I dug into my purse to grab mine, and then I grabbed Gracie's out of her hand and handed it to the bitch.

"How are you beautiful ladies doing today?" The supervisor asked, trying to start a small conversation, as we waited on our visitors' pass and the room number.

"I'm doing well, thanks," Gracie replied.

"I'm doing great as well, now that I'm actually being helped like I'm supposed to.

The supervisor looked at me with a baffled look.

"Did you have a bad day today?" She asked.

The rude receptionist looked up at me, once more. I looked at her, and then I looked over at the supervisor and said, "Well, you know, today isn't the issue. The other day was."

She looked at me and said, "What do you mean?"

"I was here a few days ago, inquiring about my child's father's room number. He had gotten shot with my kid in the car with him and I had no clue where they were. I found out everything I needed from my friend here. I was concerned and stressed, as I hadn't seen my child since I laid down to take a nap. I stood exactly where I am today. I asked this young lady, very respectfully, for help but she was a bitch about it. It seemed as if she didn't want to work and sat her ass right in that seat she hopped out of today because you are standing here."

I continued, "I just need to know, ma'am, do y'all allow y'all's employees to behave that way?"

"No, ma'am, we don't," the supervisor said, in a stern voice, turning to look at the receptionist.

"I sincerely apologize for the experience you had, and I want you to know that it will be taken care of by me personally. That is truly unacceptable, and I can ensure you that you will not have this issue again."

She asked for my name and number to contact me about the situation. She handed me a piece of scrap paper and said, "I'm Marla; my direct office number and name is here. If you have any issues, please, don't hesitate to give me a call. Again, I truly apologize."

"You haven't done anything wrong. You have been a great help," I said to the supervisor, looking over at the receptionist.

"Go on, apologize to this young lady," she ordered the receptionist.

She looked at me, angrily, with a frown and rolled her eyes. "I'm sorry," she said.

I went over to her, stood directly in front of her, and looked her in the eyes. "I don't think it was genuine, but I guess it's acceptable."

"I'm so sorry, ma'am. We won't hold y'all up much longer. Here are your IDs. The room number is 405. Just go around the corner here." She pointed. "Take elevator A to the fourth floor. When you get off the elevator, make a right and it's gon' be on your left. Again, ladies, I do apologize and have a wonderful day."

Gracie grabbed the IDs from her and smiled. "Thank you so much," she told them. We walked along the quiet halls to the elevator. Gracie looked at me and I looked at her. She busted out laughing and so did I.

"Why did you do that?" She asked.

"She had it coming for being a bitch to me. Besides, humor is good for the soul. We needed that. Did you see the look on her face the entire time?" I joked.

"I did. You've gotten that girl in some deep, deep shit. You are so petty!" Gracie said.

"I'll take that as a compliment," I laughed.

"Why is she here?" I asked, referring to Chanel.

"Girl, you would not even believe why," Gracie said.

"Tell me. Is she going into labor?"

"No, but it's definitely about the baby."

I snatched Gracie by the arm and stopped her before we got to the room. "I don't want to see their baby, Gracie. I know I'm not ready for that. I'll take the kids and sit in the car; I'm not doing that."

"Shhh..." Gracie said to me, as I was loud, in the seemingly quiet hallway.

"She had a miscarriage. She lost a lot of blood and fainted. She was rushed here and doesn't have anyone else. She asked that I come. Please, be on your best behavior."

"Wow! Damn! That's fucked up," I replied.

"Yeah, it is. So, please, Tara, I'm begging you."

"Alright, alright."

Gracie knocked on the door to the room, and then she led us in. She went to hug Chanel and I did as well.

"Thank y'all so much for coming. Especially, you, Tara. I know things have gotten crazy between us and I regret a lot that I have done to you, said to you, and the way I treated you. I hate that I can't take any of it back," Chanel cried.

I was lost for words. As a grown-ass woman, she was well aware of what she did and the decisions that she made, but here she lie, sincerely begging for sympathy and forgiveness. I stood in the room with my arms crossed. The room was as quiet as a mouse - besides the beeping sounds from the machines.

I was dying to say how I felt about what she said. I wanted to forget the conversation Gracie and I had before entering the room seconds prior. Gracie stared at me. I mugged Chanel, and with baby girl on my lap, I stared out the window, not responding to anything she said.

Gracie looked at me and said, "Tara, she's trying, come on."

Before I could speak, Chanel replied, "It's fine, Gracie. I know this isn't something that will be fixed overnight. She needs time and I get it. I would too."

Then, Chanel looked at me and said, "Tara, I just want you to know I miss you and will do whatever it takes to get our friendship how it used to be."

I mumbled under my breath, "Bitch, it will never be the same."

Gracie cleared her throat and said, "I think there is hope, y'all. I love it. We are all talking like grown women, instead of fussing and fighting like hood rats."

"Yeah, for now," I chimed in.

Chanel rolled her eyes.

Gracie changed the conversation and started asking her how she was feeling. She was finally focusing on the real reason we were sitting here.

"I'm doing ok, I guess."

"What happened? You never told me," Gracie said.

"I was at the house with Norris and we were sitting in the living room, as I vented to him about me and Chris. I wondered what my next move would be for me and the baby, since Chris had no intentions on helping me get on my feet. Shortly after, I started cramping and got the urge to pee. I got up and went in the bathroom. I sat on the toilet and the pain got worse."

Chanel continued, "I didn't know what was going on. I knew immediately that it wasn't normal. I was in tears. Norris wasn't much help, since he'd just got out the hospital himself. I yelled to him from the bathroom to call the EMS. By the time they got there, blood was all over me and in the toilet. The pain had eased up just a little but there the baby was. Right there in the toilet. I never flushed until they got there. I stood in the bathroom, holding my vagina and staring in the toilet, in shock that I was having a miscarriage."

Then, Chanel told Gracie that she hadn't spoken to Chris until yesterday, when she called to tell him about what happened.

"I'm sure he's happy this happened. He seemed like he didn't want this anyway," she cried.

Gracie got up and stood alongside Chanel's bed, wiping her tears.

"Girl, let me tell you something. God knows what's best for all of us. He never makes any mistakes. This wasn't for y'all.

This was your way out. If it was meant to be, it would have been. The baby and the relationship," she told Chanel.

Chanel started crying hysterically. Gracie stood for a while, comforting her. I sat there, hoping to leave soon, because I didn't care to be there in the first place. I texted Daddy the entire time I sat there, until there was a knock at the door.

"Are you expecting someone?" Gracie asked.

"No," Chanel replied, in a frightened voice.

I know I had a lot of shit going on myself with Norris and Anthony's brother, so I was paranoid as hell. Gracie went to the door to see who it was, and I peeped behind the curtain. I hoped and prayed nothing crazy was getting ready to pop off - once again - in this damn hospital.

We heard a man's voice. He acknowledged Gracie and all I saw was his arms, as she leaned out the door to hug him. She welcomed him in. I realized that it was Chris and his homeboy, Andrew, '*The business partner.*' I wasn't expecting to see his ass again so soon.

Chris looked at me, looked at baby girl, and then said, "Sup, Tara?"

It was awkward as hell in the room. Gracie went back over to Chanel, while Chris went over and gave her a hug.

"How you feelin'?" He asked.

"I'll be ok," she told him.

"Do you need anything?"

"Nothing that you're willing to give me," she replied.

"What do you mean? What are you talking about?"

"I need money, Chris. I barely have a place to stay 'cause I ain't got shit."

"Calm down, Chanel," Gracie chimed in.

"Fuck this nigga, Gracie. I don't even know what his purpose was for showing up. He doesn't give a fuck about me. This is probably what he wanted. He probably only came here to see for himself that it was true."

Just when I wanted to walk out, things were starting to heat up. This time, I wasn't getting in the middle of shit. I couldn't believe how Chris was treating Chanel. That wasn't the man I dated. He changed after we got married, but he seemed to love her when we were in the courtroom.

Chanel continued, "Tell me, Chris, why are you here? You and that disrespectful motherfucker who didn't even have the decency to say hi or ask if I was ok. He doesn't give a fuck either."

"Listen, I didn't come here for all of this drama. That's why I left your ass where I left you. Since you wanna know so badly; yeah, I came down here to check on you… and yes, I came to see if it was real. Since it is, I'm glad I can finally cut ties with you, so we can live happily ever after."

"We? I don't want your ass after you left me," Chanel said, loudly.

"I don't want your ass either! I wasn't talking about you," Chris replied. He went behind the curtain towards the door. When he came from behind the curtain, he held Andrew's hand. Andrew stood beside Chris, uncomfortably. I sat there confused as well.

"So, *we* can live happily ever after," Chris said.

"I knew something wasn't right when we had our threesomes. Y'all were more into it than I was. So, tell me this… How long have y'all been fuckin' around?" Chanel asked.

"Yeah, tell me too, because I need to know!" I said.

Chris looked at the both of us and said, "The entire time we were together."

"The entire time who was together?" I asked, as I sat baby girl in the chair I slowly got up from.

"Tara!" Gracie yelled.

"Almost the entire time I was with you and the entire time I was with her," he looked at me and said.

Chanel laid in the bed, silently, as I took over. Not for her, but for me. I was now finding out that my ex-husband was in love with a man. The man he said was his business partner. He was possibly laid up with this guy, while he claimed to love me, while we were married and after. When I was home alone, raising the child we thought was his, he was in Atlanta, living the life he always wanted with a man that meant more to him than we did. Why did he propose to me when that's not what he wanted? Was I just his coverup until he was ready to come out of the closet?

"Your nasty-ass picked a man over me?" I asked.

"Tara, it ain't like that. We weren't sure if this was what we wanted at first," Chris explained.

"Fuck you, Chris! You are a nasty-ass nigga. If you're gay, let it be known. You were too ashamed to be yourself, so you decided to hurt motherfuckers who showed you genuine love," I said to him, shaking my head.

I continued, "You need help, brah! For real. I'm glad we are done and divorced. This shit is sick. I can't believe…you know what? Never mind."

"Tara, I always loved you, for real."

"Did you really?" I asked, sarcastically…

"Now, Chris? Why did you have to do this now? Why here? Don't you think enough is going on? You are wrong for this…you are wrong!" Gracie said.

Chanel started crying and hollered, "Get out! Get the fuck out, Chris! Take you and your…whatever he is… with you! I never want to see you again."

The babies started crying and the machine started beeping loudly. Chris and Andrew left out and nurses rushed in.

"I need everyone to exit the room," one of the nurses hollered.

I grabbed the babies and started walking out.

"What's going on?" Gracie asked.

"Is she ok? Talk to me. Tell me something," Gracie hollered, as she was forced out of the room.

"Chanel, call me. Call me, Chanel, please."

Chanel never responded, and the nurses pushed Gracie out the door. We walked down the hall, as more nurses and doctors ran down the hall to the room yelling, "Code blue."

After I got home and washed up, I laid in the bed. Daddy hadn't gotten home yet, and baby girl was asleep. I thought about how fucked up the day was. Finding out, with everyone else, that my ex-husband was cheating on me with a man the entire time we were married, was not only mortifying but disgusting as well.

That time when he said that it was Andrew's chocolate syrup, the time when he showed interest in trying anal, the used tube of lube, and how he acted while he was doing it made me believe that he was boo'd up with Andrew all those times he was in Atlanta for work. I argued over and over that he was dealing with other women, but I'm convinced that there were more men than women. Who would have ever thought that I would be cheated on for a damn man?

Chapter 14

"I'm No Fool"

I sat on the kitchen counter with Daddy standing between my legs. I hugged him, holding him tightly and kissed all over him, as I thanked him for being there with us. Finding out what I did at the hospital a few days ago had my head fucked up.

I never told Daddy what happened, but with the baby fever I had lately, I took that time to talk to him about it. I wanted to see where his head was, and I hoped that he would agree.

"Daddy, I love you," I told him.

He grabbed my face and stared in my eyes, as he told me he loved me too.

"I've been thinking."

"About what?" He asked.

"More kids. I've had baby fever for a while now. What do you think about us trying? I'm ready for us to have our first kid together."

"Baby, we already have our kid together. Armani is all we need right now. You're always busy and I am too. With another kid, our lives will be hectic. More than it is already."

I was saddened by the response I got from him. I expected him to be excited about it, just as much as I was. I hopped off the counter and ran to the room. He followed behind me.

"Baby? Baby!" he yelled.

"Just leave me alone," I hollered.

I balled up in the bed with baby girl who was now awake from all the noise we made.

"I want a kid too. Just not right now," Daddy explained.

"So, you want kids, just not with me?" I cried.

He came over to me, leaned on the bed, grabbed me and kissed me. "That's not what I'm saying at all."

"So, what are you saying?" I asked.

"Now is just not a good time."

Devastated by how the entire conversation went, I threw on some clothes, grabbed baby girl and headed out the door. I planned to go for a ride to clear my head. Then, something came to me. I called up baby girl's sitter and dropped her off.

I picked up my phone and went through my contacts, as I walked back to my car.

"Are you busy?" I asked.

"No, what's good?"

"Can we meet up?" I asked, again.

"Yeah, I'm at the hotel. Can you come now?"

"Are you alone?"

"For right now, yes."

"Which one are you at?" I asked him.

"Hawthorn Suites on West Park. Room 228."

"Cool. I'm just around the corner. I'll be there in five minutes."

I walked in the hotel, and went to the second floor, searching for room 228. I knocked on the door and Chris answered. He gave me a hug and I looked around to be sure that I was safe, because no one knew where I was.

"So, what's going on?"

"That's what I'm here to find out. That was fucked up how we all found out about your situation; especially, me. I don't know about anybody else, but I didn't deserve to find out like that. I don't care too much for Chanel, but she didn't deserve that either. There's some things I'd like to know."

"So, was I just a coverup?" I continued.

"I'm glad you're here. I didn't want to tell y'all like that, but you don't know what Chanel and I went through. I was fed up with her. She's cheated on me, lied to me, even stole from me. You don't know the half of what we've been through. I had to let her know that we were finally done. I was tired."

"Well, that's definitely your karma," I mumbled.

"What y'all did to me was foul," I told him.

"I know it was. She was throwing herself at me, so I wanted to try her. It was supposed to be a hit and quit thing, but it never stopped."

"And she was willing to do things that you weren't. I liked the excitement she brought in the bedroom," Chris continued.

"Ok, just stop. I don't want to hear that shit."

"Now, y'all wanna come running back to me for help and support but I don't know how y'all expect me to be so easy on y'all."

"I don't think neither one of us wanted to lose your friendship, after realizing how fucked up it all was. I still love you, don't get me wrong."

I stared out the window, as I started to get emotional. *I didn't come here for this*, I thought.

Changing the subject, I started talking about what brought me there.

"So, are you gay or bisexual?"

"I like both, but I prefer men."

"How long have you been bisexual?"

"I tried guys back in high school, and then went back to girls. If you are wondering, Andrew and I really were just friends when you and I started dating. After we opened up the club and started spending more time together, we started messing around on the low."

"I don't know what to say," I told Chris.

"So, tell me the truth about the chocolate syrup I found and the lube you had that was half used," I demanded.

Then, I asked another question when he started speaking. "So, that's the reason you wanted anal that night?"

Chris started sweating heavily and rubbing his head with both hands. He always did that when he was really nervous.

"Ok… alright…this is it. So, I did tell the truth about the chocolate syrup. It was Andrews, but he didn't leave it the night all the guys were at the house chillin'. He left it after he used it on me. The lube was from us as well. And the anal... I wanted sex that night, but I like fucking assholes more, so that's why I begged you to do it. You are the only woman I've asked to do that, though."

"Lucky me," I said, sarcastically.

Chris continued, "We did spend a lot of nights together. He was over at the house a lot and I was over at his. We went out together and we did a lot of shit in that house, but we never did anything in the bedroom you and I shared."

"Is that supposed to make me feel better? You probably didn't do anything with him in there, but you did other bitches in that room for sure," I argued.

"Let's not go there, Tara," Chris replied.

"Why not?" I asked.

My stomach turned multiple times. I threw up in my mouth a little bit, but I knew for sure that wasn't all. I ran in the bathroom and let the rest out in the toilet. I was so sick to my stomach, after what Chris told me. The situation with Chris and Andrew was disgusting. There was no way in hell this could be my reality right now.

Chris came in the bathroom to check on me.

"I'm ok...I'm ok." I told him. I stopped him from touching me and stood in the mirror, wiping the rest of the vomit off of my mouth with a napkin.

He led me to the bed to sit. I sat on the edge of the bed where I was before. He looked at me and said, "Tara, I'm not telling you this to hurt you. I never wanted to hurt you, but maybe I am fucked up in the head like you said. I want us to have closure. We don't have to be friends, but we don't have to hate each other either. I told you this, so that we both can move on. Growing up, I always heard my mom saying, 'We're only as sick as our secrets' and I never thought anything of it… until I realized… I realized how much you meant to me and how bad I hurt you. You are a good woman. I appreciate the chance I had to love and be with you. Please, don't let my dumbass mistakes fuck you up from allowing yourself to be loved by a man you deserve."

He stared at me, after speaking, and all I could do was listen. I didn't say anything. I didn't have any more tears to shed and I felt lighter, as if a huge weight was lifted off of my shoulders. I knew that was what I needed. The fact that I couldn't cry, I knew I was moving on. I didn't hate him, but we couldn't be friends so soon. I needed time to heal myself and move when I was ready, for once, instead of when I was told to.

"Umm… I think I should get going," I told Chris.

Chris grabbed his phone to look at the time and replied, "Yeah … umm… ok."

"Can I get a hug?" He asked.

I stopped, looked at him and walked out the door.

After picking up baby girl, I phoned Gracie while we drove home. We talked a little bit about what went down at the hospital. She told me that she'd just left from seeing Chanel and that she was doing fine. She told me that the code blue was due to her blood pressure rising so high. That was to be expected. Chris came in there and kicked her in the back while she was already down. Hell, after what he said, I'm sure he raised my blood pressure too.

She was already stressed out and grieving over a baby she carried but would never be able to meet. Not to mention, Chris wasn't supportive at all. He was a fucked-up individual. A crazy-ass man, and thankfully, he was no longer mine.

When I stepped foot in the condo, I put Armani down to run wild and I saw fresh, red, rose petals all over the floor that led to the dining room table. I followed the trail. Daddy had set the table beautifully. He decorated the table with flowers in a vase and he had a bottle of champagne waiting for me. He knew I was upset, before I walked out, and was trying to make up for it.

"What are you cookin'?" I asked, walking up behind him to hug and kiss him on the cheeks.

"Hey, baby. Just something simple, nothing big tonight. I have wild rice, string beans and fried pork chops."

"Mmm… sounds and smells delicious," I told him, while I walked in the bathroom.

"I gotta make sure my little princess and my favorite queen eats," he yelled from the kitchen, but I could hear him coming closer to me.

"*Favorite?*" I hollered back.

He walked up behind me, as I stood in the mirror, making sure no dried tears were on my face. He kissed me on my cheek and neck and said, "My only." Then, he kissed me some more.

I turned around and faced him, as we continued to tongue each other down. He stopped for a second, peeped out to the living room to make sure baby girl was good, and then closed the bathroom door behind him.

He pulled my panties down, lifted me on the bathroom counter where my pretty, plump ass cheeks sat and stood between my legs while he dropped his jeans and boxers.

"I need it, Daddy. Give…"

Before I could finish my sentence, he was sliding inside me.

"Did you miss Daddy?"

"Yeessss!" I hollered.

I moaned, loudly, as I rubbed across his well-built, toned body.

"Let's make a baby," I hollered.

"You wanna baby?" He asked.

"Yes, Daddy, yes! Oh, yes, Daddy!" I moaned.

We were getting into it. He was in me deeply. Then, we heard a knock at the door.

We kept going, but the longer we went, the louder the knocks got. Whoever it was, pounded as if they were the police. I ignored it, as I tried to focus on what we had going on, but I could see that Daddy wasn't able to concentrate anymore.

"I'm gonna get the door, then we can finish," He said, while he still stroked me.

"No, Daddy, please! Don't stop!" I moaned. I wrapped my arms around his back, pulling him closer to me.

We still heard the knocking, and then baby girl started crying. Daddy pulled out, slid on his underwear and pants, leaving me sitting on the counter, and told me he would be back to finish.

"Who?" He asked, walking towards the door.

I could hardly hear anything, with Armani crying, but I didn't want to get up either because we weren't done.

He left the bathroom door slightly cracked, so I saw him walk to the door and open it, but I didn't see who it was on the other side. He stepped outside the door and closed the door behind him. I sat on the counter for about three minutes more, then I got dressed, washed my hands and left out.

Baby girl was still hollering, so I went to comfort her. I rocked her, and she ended up falling asleep shortly after. I laid her in the playpen and went to see what Daddy had going on.

He was taking some time and I was worried that he stepped out and hadn't come back in yet. I couldn't hear or see him, so I went to the door. Before opening the door, I put my ear to it and heard whispering. I opened the door to see what was going on and what all the whispering was about.

As soon as I opened the door, they both looked at me. He was outside the door, talking to the realtor bitch, Asia. She was not dressed like she was working, and I didn't understand why she was here.

"What's going on?" I asked.

The realtor looked at me funny and started speaking, but then Daddy cut her off quickly and said, "Baby, it's all good. Go 'head back inside, I'll be right behind you in a few."

I stood there with my arms crossed. I eyed her up and down and said, "Are you sure everything's good?"

"Yes, baby, everything is ok."

"Why is she here?" I asked.

"Well..." the realtor started speaking, but then Daddy cut her off, again.

"I'll explain when I come inside."

"No, I'm not a fuckin' fool. If it's nothing, go ahead and continue the conversation y'all were having before I stepped out here."

"Yeah, Anthony, continue. Tell her!"

"Tell me what?" I asked, curiously.

Anthony didn't say anything. The realtor continued, "I'm pregnant."

"By who? You are the realtor, what the fuck does that have to do with us?" I asked.

"Girl, is you dumb? If it ain't had nothing to do with him, do you think I would be standing here right now?"

I looked at Anthony and snatched his ass up quickly.

"Let's go! Get your ass in the damn house," I told him, snatching and grabbing on him.

When we got inside, I slammed the door on her.

Chapter 15

"The Truth Lies Beneath"

"So, this is the same chick that you told me was a homegirl, right? Somebody that you knew and grew up with, but y'all have been sleeping together? What's really going on, Anthony? I told you from the beginning I didn't have time for games. You know what I went through."

I continued, "To make the situation worse, you introduced me to this bitch. And you told me you didn't want kids, but you have her pregnant!"

"Man, Tara, listen, it ain't even like that."

"So, what's it like, Anthony? Tell me what it is and don't beat around the bush. Tell me everything, now!" I hollered.

"I told you the truth, baby. She wanted me when we were growing up, but as we got older, she no longer showed interest in me. The entire time I was single, before me and you even met, she never came on to me. We slept together once or twice or maybe even three times, but there were no strings attached. We never dated. There were no feelings involved - so I thought - and we both were fine with that. She wasn't seeing anyone, and I wasn't seeing anyone. That was a while ago, though. If she had gotten pregnant when we messed around, she would have been farther along than she is now."

"So, why would she make this up, Anthony? Please, explain it to me."

"She's probably in her feelings because we are dealing with each other and we are happy. I talk to her often about how happy you make me and how good our relationship is. I also told her before how I wish I met you a long time ago, so she probably grew jealous hearing those things. She always had issues with finding the right men."

"So, when y'all talked, y'all have never mentioned anything about being together or being in love?"

"No, baby, I swear! She's not even my type. We've never been on a date and never hung out without being with other people. I'm being real, I don't know where this is coming from. I'm just as shocked as you are. I'm just as confused. I would not let anyone come between what we have and where we will be or where we are going. I will get to the bottom of this."

Damn, I was so confused. What he was saying sounded real. Like he didn't give a fuck about this woman. Like he didn't know what the hell was going on or why she would do such a thing to him. But men these days were sneaky as hell. They would do whatever they needed and say whatever they had to get out of the situation that had them stuck. I didn't know what to say or what to believe, at this point.

"If all of this is true, I don't know if I trust you talking to her or being around her alone anymore. I need to be there. I want you to block this bitch. Anytime she pops up on you, I need to know that too. Now that I know it's more to it than just a '*long time friendship.*' I'm serious about what I'm saying Anthony."

"I understand, baby. I don't blame you for feeling this way and I promise to let you know about everything. I don't want this to cause conflict in our relationship. I promise! You have my word on that."

"Can we finish what we were doing?" Daddy asked.

"I am not really in the mood anymore, to be honest. This has really fucked my head up."

Daddy didn't take no for an answer. He got up from the chair he was sitting in and came to me. He started kissing all over my cheeks and face, as he did before. Then, he picked me up and took me to the bedroom. He placed me on the bed and told me to get naked. I sat on the bed, fully clothed, as he was already naked.

"What the fuck are you doing?" he asked me.

"I told you I'm not in the mood," I reminded him.

Then, he got on top of me and told me he would be putting his dick in something, even if it wasn't my pussy.

All I thought to myself was, *here goes this gay shit again*. I assumed that he was talking about my asshole. And then, he brought his dick by my face and shoved it in my mouth, leaving me no way to say no I didn't want to do it. I did what I had to do, and by the time I was done, I wanted sex, again.

I started undressing myself, as I deep throated him. He knew, for sure, I would change my mind after doing that.

"That's my girl," he said.

I rolled my eyes at him and told him to make it quick.

He pushed me down on the bed and threw my legs in the air over his shoulders.

"Who does this dick belong to, girl?" He asked.

I just moaned and took what he was giving me, not answering the question that he asked. Truth was, after what I'd just saw and heard, I didn't know the answer to that question anymore.

He went harder and asked again, but I still didn't speak. I just moaned louder.

Then, he went even harder and asked again, and this time I started to say me, but then he nutted and pulled out.

I laid on the bed, holding my pussy, and then he came and laid behind me.

"I love you," he whispered, while he rubbed on my sore pussy he tore apart moments before.

"Be gentle, it hurts," I told him.

"I'm sorry, baby. I just wanted you to know that this dick belongs to you and only you."

I didn't say anything, which led him to ask, "Do you believe me?"

I stayed quiet and then I finally said, "Mmhmm."

I felt like it was an obstacle course I couldn't get out of. He had never lied to me. He was always open about any and everything he did; because without a doubt, he loved me.

After a few days of Daddy showing me affection, I distorted my mind into believing what happened with the realtor was all a lie. Shit, to be honest, ol' girl couldn't compete. No way would he pick her lame-ass over me.

Daddy had been working a lot lately. With the girls doing so good at the boutique, I was able to fall back from it more and be a full-time mommy - for the most part. Often, I found myself bored and not wanting to be alone in the house. Gracie was the only friend I had left, and now that she wasn't working, we chilled together a lot.

Since I was alone and bored, I went over to Gracie's to chill with her for a while. We sat at the kitchen table, playing cards, while drinking our wine after the kids fell asleep. Josh was out, so we had the place all to ourselves to cut up and act a fool if we wanted to.

I was rusty on the card game; I hadn't played in a while. After getting my ass whooped over and over, we called it quits and sat at the table, while I scrolled on Instagram on my phone and she scrolled on Facebook on hers.

After about four minutes of her being on Facebook, I heard a lot of noise on her phone.

"What the hell is going on over there?" I asked.

"I'm trying to figure out now. Ya boy is on Live, acting a fool."

"My boy?" I was confused by what she said because Anthony didn't have social media. I started to wonder if she knew something I didn't. I got up from my chair and went over to her, quickly, to see what she was talking about.

When I went over to her, Norris was on her screen. I immediately rolled my eyes. Inattentive to the bullshit he was talking about, I went back to the opposite side of the table where I had been.

I went back on Instagram, as Gracie continued to watch his Facebook Live, not giving me a choice but to listen to what was going on. He started talking and cursing.

"Damn, he's pissed off about something," Gracie said.

"I'm sure he is," I mumbled.

"Have y'all talked lately?"

"Hell no! I told you he has too much shit going on. I don't have time for any of it. I'm not going back on my word, this time."

"I don't blame you. I can tell," she said, holding up her phone."

As soon as Gracie started to say, "I'm clicking off of this," I told her not too and ran back over.

"Gracie, wait. Hold up, let me see your phone!"

Norris was on the Facebook Live saying, "Yeah, nigga, I know it was you. My baby mama probably had something to do with it. Y'all want me dead, but you fuckin' missed. Watch y'all back, nigga… Watch y'all back."

I looked at Gracie and she looked back at me, but I didn't say anything. I immediately thought about Anthony's brother when I heard him say that. I wasn't sure if he knew that it was Anthony's brother who did that to him. It sounded like he felt like I set him up, which I didn't. Then, I thought, *what if Anthony's brother saw his Facebook Live and thought I tipped Norris off about what they did and what he said to me.* Maybe I was overthinking shit, but there was no time to sit there and figure out.

"What is he talking about, Tara?"

"I don't know," I told her.

"Are you lying? Is this why you aren't around him anymore?"

"No, Gracie, I'm not lying." I grabbed my keys, my purse and my kid, right before running out the door. All I said to her was, "I gotta go!"

Five minutes after I left Gracie's, she started calling me, but I didn't answer. Soon as my phone stopped ringing, it started back. It was still her. She kept calling back. Then, she texted me and the text read, "Are you ok?" Then, another text came through right after that said, "Norris saw I was on his Live and now he's asking where you are. What should I tell him?"

I called her back and said, "I can't say much right now, but don't tell him anything about me, Anthony or Armani."

"You're scaring me. Please, talk to me."

"I can't right now, but I might need to go away for a couple of days. I left a set of keys on your counter next to your stove. Those are the spare keys to my apartment and the store. I might need you to watch over the store for me. If you call and I don't answer, I will text you when I can. I love you."

"I love you more, girl."

Chapter 16

"What Did You Do?"

W hen I got home that night, I laid in the bed with Armani tucked under me, and Daddy on the other side. I had plans to wake up early, pack some of my things and take baby girl away for a week or so. The conversation Anthony's brother had with me at the hospital and what Norris said on his Facebook Live terrified me. I knew we were in danger and shouldn't stick around much longer. I couldn't turn to anyone for help because it could make things worse, and that unsettled me more.

I could hardly sleep. I tossed and turned all night, lying in the dark room, looking up at the ceiling, listening to the two of them snore in my ears, as if they were having the best sleep they've ever had, but I couldn't seem to find. I looked at the clock over and over again, only to see it read 1:46am and I'd been in bed since 9pm. *Damn, times going by slow*, I thought to myself.

Since I couldn't sleep, I got up and went in the living room to watch some TV. I hoped that I would finally get sleepy and pass out, before having to wake up in a few hours. I went in the living room, turned the TV on, and as soon as I got back up to go get a glass of orange juice, there was a knock at my door.

It startled me because so much had been going on, and I wasn't expecting anyone. I stood in the middle of the floor, without making a move, after the first knock. I prayed that since nobody answered, that whomever it was would walk away and leave. Instead, they kept knocking.

I ran in the room, trying to keep as quiet as I could, so I wouldn't wake baby girl, and so whoever it was at the door didn't hear me.

"Daddy!" I whispered.

"Anthony," I continued, as I shook him.

"Huh?" He mumbled.

"Somebody's at the door!"

"Who is it?" He asked, jumping up.

"I don't know, but I'm scared!"

"What time is it?"

"It's 2:10am."

"It's 2:10 in the morning?" He asked.

"Yes, hurry!"

Daddy hopped out the bed, rubbing his eyes. He went in the closet, reached on the top shelf and pulled down the Nike shoe box where we kept our guns. He had a 9mm, semi-automatic, chrome, 92 series Beretta that I thought he was grabbing; but instead, I saw him walking out of the room with my pink beauty. He added bullets to the clip, loaded it and went to the door.

I started to question why he took my gun; but if we really were in danger, it didn't matter, as long as we were safe. I stayed behind and stayed quiet. I stood behind my cracked room door, as I peeped out to see and hear what was going on. Daddy walked up to the door and asked, "Who is it," while he peeped through the peephole. The person didn't speak, so Daddy asked again. The person pounded on the door harder.

I started to get concerned about all the noise that was being made. I had neighbors close by in the condo and I didn't want any issues. Daddy opened the door and it was Norris.

"Norris?" I said, quietly to myself.

"What do you want?" Daddy asked furiously.

Norris walked in the condo and said, "Revenge, fool. I know you and your peoples had something to do with me getting shot."

"Listen, brah, I don't know what the hell you are talking about and I want you out my damn house," Daddy said, still standing with the door wide open.

"Word on the street is you were the motherfucker that shot me. Yeah, I know about you, nigga."

"Listen, get out! There is no reason for you to be here right now!" Daddy hollered, as his voice got deeper.

I stepped out of the room into the living room where they stood, closing the bedroom door behind me.

"Norris, what the fuck are you doing here?" I asked.

"Where's my daughter, Tara? I wanna see my daughter!"

"Norris, I told you not to contact us or come by until you got your shit together."

"Go back in the room, Tara!" Anthony yelled.

Daddy started walking towards Norris, slowly, with his gun behind his back. "Listen, brah, I'm only going to tell you one more time to leave."

Norris refused to leave. Instead, he started walking around my place, looking for Armani. He went towards my room, where she actually was, and then I heard a gunshot.

I stood where I was standing and screamed loudly, as my ears rung badly! I couldn't believe what Anthony had just done.

Norris started stumbling, while he held his chest and breathed heavily. Next thing I knew, he was on the floor, right before my eyes. I ran over to him, crying hysterically. Norris looked at me, while he continued to hold his chest and gasp in agony for air. He moaned and groaned in extreme pain. He held my arm and tried squeezing it, but he didn't have much strength. About six minutes after watching him suffer, his hand loosened on my arm and dropped down to the floor.

I shook Norris and yelled, "Wake up! Get up! Norris! No! Open your eyes! Wake up!"

I looked over to Anthony, yelling, "What did you do? What the fuck did you just do? Why...why did you shoot him? You didn't have to kill him!"

On my knees next to him, his blood got thicker around my feet and ran along the cracks of my once-sparkling, clean, hardwood floors. I touched his body while it was still warm. I stared at him while he still looked like himself and I held his hands while I still had the chance to.

"What you standing there for? Do something!" I told Anthony.

He went to grab my phone and called 911. I refused to leave Norris' side, until I heard Armani crying. She was sitting in the middle of the bed, crying, awakened by the loud noise and scared of the darkness that filled the bedroom.

I went over to her and grabbed her, spreading all of Norris' blood all over her light pink onesie that read, My Daddy Loves Me.

"Shhh... baby! It's ok! Mommy's here. I got you," I whispered to her, shaking her to calm her down, as I hoped that it would calm me as well. I put my hand on the back of her head, pushing her head down on my shoulder.

"I got you! Mommy's here now."

I stood in the room with Armani and then I heard a knock at the room door. I was already shaken up from what happened. The loud knock on the bedroom door startled me more because it sounded as loud as the gunshot that went off. It scared the life out of me.

"Baby, I'm sorry; I didn't mean to scare y'all. Are y'all ok?"

"I don't know, Anthony! I really don't know. What did you do?" I cried.

"I'm sorry, baby! I was trying to protect y'all."

"Ok... just leave me alone for a while. I need some time."

"The neighbors are out here, worried, and asking questions. Do you want to talk to them?"

"NO! I don't have anything to say!"

"Ok, baby... But, what do you want me to tell them?"

"Something...anything! Tell them we are fine; we just had an intruder. I don't know! Figure it out, please. And give me my phone."

I texted Gracie and told her to come over ASAP! I knew she would probably be asleep, so I called her. The phone rung and I didn't get an answer. I waited a minute and tried calling again.

"Please, pick up, please, pick up," I whispered.

"Gracie? Thank God you answered."

"Is everything ok, Tara?"

"No, Gracie, it's not! Please, come over to my place… and hurry!"

"Josh and I will be right over."

I started packing some clothes for me and Armani to give to Gracie - once she got here. I didn't know what was going to happen next. Would I be going to jail because my gun was used? Would my child get taken from me? Where would I stay if I didn't go to jail? I was shaking badly. I was nervous and scared about everything that could happen to me.

Shortly after I was done packing, the emergency officials arrived. They started talking to us and asking us a lot of questions. They walked through the house, looking around and taking pictures. They took my gun, threw up some caution tape and covered the body.

"I'm going to need you both down at the station. Is there anyone that can come get the kid?" The officer asked me.

"Uh, yes. I called for my sister to come and get her; she should be on the way," I replied, looking at my phone.

I had a miss call from Gracie.

"She called me. Is it ok that I call her back?" I asked the officer.

"Sure, just stand here," he told me.

I called her back. She told me that she was downstairs, and the police would not let her up. I told him where she was, and the officer walked down with me, so I could hand Armani over to her.

"What's going on, Tara?" Gracie asked me.

"Not right now. I'll talk to you about it later," I told her, handing baby girl to her.

They put me in cuffs and then in the backseat of the police car. I sat in the backseat of the police car, for the very first time, crying. And then, I saw Daddy coming out of the building in cuffs as well. He went in a separate police car.

They took us down to the station. After going through the entire process with the police, we were finally released three hours later. We called an Uber to take us to my place to grab a car. We ended up taking Daddy's car and were headed over to Gracie's, because we couldn't stay at home. Then, Daddy said he was stopping by his brothers' house.

That was the last place I wanted to be, besides the police station. I didn't want to go, and I also didn't understand why this was a necessary stop to make at 6am. I started to put up a fuss about it, but then I kept cool. I wanted to eavesdrop on their conversation and find out where his brothers lived. In all the time we'd been talking, he never took me over to their place.

I sat on the passenger side of his darkly-tinted, silver, 2018 Jaguar XF. He had five percent black tint on it, so the car was dark as hell, from the outside looking in. They would never be able to tell that I was inside the car. I'm sure they would never think he would bring me there anyway.

"I'll stay in the car when you make your stop," I told him.

"That's fine, baby. I know it makes you uncomfortable being around them. I was going to have you stay in the car anyway."

"Mmm… ok!" I said.

"How long is this going to take? We've been up all night and I need some rest."

"I won't be long, baby. Give me a kiss. I love you."

He pulled along the sidewalk in front of their house. The place was huge, and they had three, foreign cars and a Chevy Tahoe in the driveway. *They have some expensive shit*, I thought, for three men that didn't punch a clock to get paid. I had money from my parents and my business, and I still couldn't afford all the shit they had and the lifestyle they lived. They must be making real money out there. *No wonder why they don't play behind it*, I thought.

When Daddy got out the car and walked up to the house, I saw his older brother walk out. That was the same one that came over and whispered in my ear at the hospital. He walked over to Daddy and dapped him up, stopping Daddy from going inside the house.

As they talked, I tried reading his brother's lips, but it was much harder than I expected. Daddy had his back to the car the entire time. His brother looked over to the car. As paranoid as I was, I started to recline my seat as much as it could go back. Daddy turned to look at the car with him for a few seconds and then they faced each other and started talking again.

I knew from the distance they were standing and the darkness of tint on the windows that he couldn't see me, but for some reason I still felt like he knew I was there. If he walked to the car, I prepared myself to hop in the driver's seat and speed off, but I didn't have to. Shortly after, his brother walked in the house and Daddy came back to the car.

Chapter 17

"Something Isn't Right"

Staying at Gracie's while we anticipated our next move wasn't a bad idea. The place was peaceful, and they opened their doors without thinking twice. They welcomed us in with open arms, which meant a lot to me. I tried keeping out of their way. Just months ago, she vented to me about how uncomfortable and unhappy her home was when they had unwanted guests before us.

I was the only one still awake. My eyes were burning badly from the lack of sleep; and although I wanted to sleep, I couldn't. I had so much on my mind. I laid in bed, thinking, as I watched the sun come up.

"Good morning, baby," Daddy said to me, followed by a long yawn and a kiss.

"Good morning, Daddy," I said, quickly.

He eased up behind me and put his dick on my butt and rested his arms on my waist. He started grinding on me, but I pushed him away, moving my body in the opposite direction.

"Damn, baby! What's wrong? We can't get a quickie in?"

I turned around and looked at him.

"You can't be serious. Are you fuckin' kidding me right now?"

"Why not?"

"Why would I? It's uncomfortable as hell for me to be fucking in here and you act like nothing just happened. I literally just watched you kill my daughter's father in my damn face a few hours ago. I watched him die. I was next to him, watching him fight for his damn life, and all you care about right now is sex. The only thing that's important to you is getting your rocks off. You are selfish, Anthony!"

"I don't like when you call me Anthony!"

"It's your fuckin' name," I said.

"No, it's not!" He argued.

"And you still don't care. Just move! Get away from me," I continued.

"Baby, I'm sorry! You know I care about you, so stop it. I know this is a tough time for you. I didn't do it on purpose. I was just trying to protect us."

I rolled my eyes and moved a little further away from him.

"Come on, baby! I love you! I'm here for you and I will be, like I have been with everything else."

"So, what's next?" I asked.

"I need to link up with…" Anthony started to say.

"What? What are you talking about?" I asked, again.

"Nothing, I was trying to see where we can go from here," he said.

"So, do you think we should move too?" I asked.

"Hell yeah! I can't have you in the condo depressed and constantly thinking about what happened in there. How are you going to heal from this if we don't?"

"Where are we going to go? It takes time to find a place and I'm not trying to be here for months. I love them and all, but I need my space," I whispered.

"I'll find us something quickly, that's nice and up to your standards. You know I have a realtor friend who can hook us up. Let me take care of this, baby. I'll call her later and handle it."

"This bitch, again. We've talked about her," I said, rolling my eyes.

"I know baby, but we need her right now," Anthony tried convincing me.

"I don't need that bitch. I'll figure things out on my own, if I have to," I told him, stubbornly.

"If you are going to call her, I want you to do it when I'm around, like I told you before!" I continued.

"I can, baby, that's not a problem. Let's do it a little later, though. It's out of her business hours, so I doubt she will answer."

"Mmhmm!" I mumbled, as I gave him the side-eye.

"What time is it?" Daddy asked.

I thought to myself, *Well, how the hell do you know it's outside of her business hours if you don't know the time right now?* But with so much going on, I didn't have time to go back and forth with this nigga. Every little thing was starting to annoy me - including him.

I grabbed my phone off the nightstand, looked at it, and turned it towards him.

"It's 7:30am, for real? Oh shit! I gotta go!" Daddy hollered, as he jumped out the bed.

"Well, where the hell do you have to go now? It's early as hell and I need you here!"

"I forgot I have to meet a client at the office."

He threw a t-shirt on, some gym shorts and his Air Force One's, grabbed his briefcase and was close to heading out the door, before he remembered he was forgetting something. He turned around, walked over to me, and gave me a kiss.

"So, you're going to meet your clients like that?" I asked, curiously.

"No, baby! I'm going to see if I can go buy or borrow a suit and shoes, since I can't go back to the house."

"So, when are you going to give me the combination to that damn briefcase?"

"I can't, baby! It's confidential! Alright, I'll see y'all later. I gotta go! Love y'all."

"Oh, it's confidential alright," I mumbled.

I was finally able to fall asleep and didn't wake up until about three that afternoon. When I woke up, I saw that Mani was missing and I started to call Anthony, but I saw the text from Gracie that said she had baby girl. Knowing that my child was ok, I took my time gathering myself, took a shower and then got dressed, before heading downstairs to get her.

When I got downstairs, Gracie was playing on the floor with our girls. I plopped on the couch and exhaled, with a sigh of relief.

"Thank you, girl," I told Gracie.

"You know it's never a problem. How you feelin'?" She asked.

"Like shit! I can't fuckin' believe what happened."

"I know, man…me either. You don't even have to tell me. It's all over the news and social media," Gracie replied.

"Word spreads fast," she continued.

"You're damn right it does," I said.

"How's Josh holding up?"

"Not well. You know they have been boys since forever, so this is going to be a tough pill to swallow, but I got him. He will be good," she said.

"My daughter is without her father, Gracie. She will not remember him. She won't ever get to spend time with him again and I feel like a part of this is my fault."

"Tara, I need for you to understand that it's nobody's fault but his. Norris should have never came there acting like that. He was under the influence of something, whether it was drugs or alcohol, but he knew better. He had some shit going on within himself that he was dealing with. I know for sure he wasn't thinking right because that's not like him. Stop faulting yourself and Anthony for what happened, because if Anthony didn't do what he did, it could have been your funeral being planned… or even baby girl's. Stop it! You can't live with this guilt!"

She stood next to me, as I sat there on the couch and she hugged me, telling me how much she loved me and would be there for us no matter what. I gathered myself and called Anthony, but he didn't answer. I hadn't spoken to him since he left earlier this morning and I didn't wake up to any calls or texts from him. It worried me too, with everything going on. I thought nothing but the worst.

I asked Gracie to babysit Armani for me, while I ran out and checked on my shop and on Daddy. She said ok, without hesitating. I caught an Uber to my place to go grab my car, and when I got there, his car wasn't there. I drove by the office where he said he worked and was meeting clients, but his car wasn't there either. I blew up his phone, leaving the office, but there was still no answer.

I got halfway down the street and turned back around. I went inside the office building and went to the desk where two, beautiful, young women stood.

"Hi. I'm looking for my fiancé's office. This is my first time here. Would you be able to point me in the right direction?"

"Hi, ma'am! Sure, what's your fiancé's name?"

"Thank you so much. His name is Anthony Parado. He's a Criminal Justice Attorney."

The ladies looked at me with a strange look and asked that I repeat his name. I did.

"Is something wrong," I asked.

"Uhh… let me just look in the system. I'm not familiar with that name, but we have gotten a lot of new staff in the last few months. He must be new."

"Umm… no, he is not. He's been here for the past six months, at least, and he did his externship here prior to joining the team," I told them, as I reached in my purse.

"Ok, ma'am, just give me a few minutes to look this up."

While she was looking at the computer, I shuffled through my purse.

"Got it," I hollered. I showed her his business card with his picture and their address on it. "This is him," I told her, holding the card up in their faces.

"Ma'am, I'm sorry to inform you, but we don't accept externs here. There isn't a Criminal Justice Attorney working here by that name, and that business card isn't legit. The company orders business cards for all the staff and they look like this," she told me, as she pulled one from off her desk.

"See, this is how all the business cards look and we also include our address, along with the suite number they occupy on the cards as well. The card you have is totally different from what we use," the young lady said to me.

I stood at the desk with a blank stare, and in brief silence.

"Ok...ok! Thank you for your time, ladies."

I stormed out of the office, swinging my hips from side to side and pounding their marbled floor with my heels. I pushed the glass double doors wide open, as I walked through and didn't try to stop them from slamming behind me.

He was a goddamn liar that just made a fool of me. He got up every day around the same time to come here. He came home around the same time every day in his suit, with his briefcase that I never once had access to or had an idea of what was inside. *There must be some mistake. This can't be right,* I told myself.

When I got in the car, I reached in my purse for my phone and tried calling him, again. There was still no answer. I decided to ride past his brothers' place where he took me earlier. I was nervous as hell, with no tint on my car and a clear view of my face, but I did it anyway.

When I came up on the street, my phone rung. I rushed to answer it, thinking it was Daddy, but instead, it was Chris. I declined the call. Then, he called right back, and I answered.

"What, nigga? This better be important. Why are you blowing up my phone?"

"Yes, Tara, it is!"

I talked to him, as I creeped up on the house. I found no cars there, not even Anthony's.

"So, what's up?" I asked him.

"I wanted to call and check on you and little mama. I heard the news."

"Yeah! It's fucked up, but we're good. Thanks for asking. How are you?"

"Not good!" Chris said.

"Well, what's going on? From the moment I answered, I could hear it in your voice that something wasn't right, but I didn't want to cross any lines and be nosy."

"Well, it's a lot going on."

"Like what? Talk to me."

"I'm not even proud of the shit I'm about to tell you right now, but I know it will eventually get out and get back to you. As a friend, I thought I would be the one you should hear it from first."

"What's going on, Chris?"

"No, you have enough going on. This can wait."

"No, it can't! Tell me now!"

"So, a few weeks ago, I found out that Andrew and I have AIDS," He confessed.

"Say what? So, he gave it to you?"

"Yep! Right after you and I separated, he was still dealing with other dudes. He fucked the wrong nigga, caught that shit and gave it to me."

"Well, I've had my checkup after being with you and I don't have anything, if you are wondering."

"Oh, good!"

"Hold up! What about Chanel?" I asked.

"I'm sure she has it too. I haven't called her yet. How should I approach her about this?"

"Wow! Damn! I don't know what to say."

"You don't have to say anything. I deserve this for fuckin' off on you," Chris cried.

"Nobody deserves this shit. Even though you did hurt me and did some fucked-up shit to me, you don't deserve it either. None of y'all do. I don't know what's the best way to tell her, but you need to say something... Sooner than later. That's fucked up, but I'm a little busy, so I have to go," I told him.

I couldn't get in touch with Anthony and I never found out where he was, so I ran by the shop for a little bit to check on things and then headed back over to Gracie's. Time was passing by and it was getting late. I'd been dealing with headaches and bullshit and just wanted to sit down, breathe and relax.

When I got back to Gracie's and walked through the door, Chanel was sitting on the couch next to her in tears. I looked at her and didn't say anything. I already knew what that was about. I went to grab my kid out the playpen, where she laid peacefully in her pajamas next to Gracie's little girl.

Chapter 18

"Stakeout"

I stayed up late, wondering where Anthony was and what he was doing. It felt like a road I'd been down before, that I vowed I would never take again. First, Norris, and then Chris and now Anthony. Damn it! What was up with these men? They could never seem to get it right. Or maybe I had issues picking the right ones.

The one man that truly loved me, I would never see again. My first love was taken from me too soon. The one man that showed me that he loved me when he said it. The guy that made sure I smiled every day and would do whatever it took to make sure it happened. I really missed my daddy.

I needed some laughter to get my mind off things. I decided to go on Facebook. There was always funny videos that went viral or one of my Facebook friends that said something stupid. I went on the web to Facebook and found 134 notifications.

I never really went on Facebook because social media wasn't my thing, unless I needed a laugh. There were too many people bashing one another or talking down on each other; and with all the deaths people shared, I didn't want anything to do with that.

Damn! 134 notifications. What was this about, though? Some negative shit, sure enough. People were commenting on my page and bashing me about Norris' death, saying how I set him up... How I was the reason he was dead and I deserved to be put in jail.

What the hell were they talking about? I didn't have anything to do with that! I didn't know that was going to happen. Hell, I didn't even know he was going to show up that night. As I scrolled down, I saw more. They started talking about Anthony and a few people even tagged him in some of the posts. They were saying that Norris and Anthony were beefing for a while, and that his hitman never came through for him, so he took matters into his own hands.

I was confused as hell. This nigga had a Facebook page all along. Other people were saying the same thing Norris did in the house before Anthony shot him. I laid there thinking, *Was Anthony a hitman the entire time? Was I in love with a criminal? No, I'm trippin'. I can't be listening to these people*, I told myself

What else was he hiding, though? People were on there bashing him about being a known killer! Hold up! This man was a Criminal Justice Attorney. How in the hell could he be a fuckin' killer? Now, they were talking nonsense. Instead of logging off, I deactivated my page. It was getting to be too much for me.

I texted Anthony and told him that the things he had been doing all day had been a little suspicious and that I didn't like it. I told him to call me ASAP and that I would be up waiting. I waited for ten minutes and I didn't get a response. I texted, again, "Listen, where the hell are you? You have been gone all day. You haven't called or checked on me and Armani. Like, what's up?"

I got a text to my phone, a second later, and then another and I kept getting text notifications consistently for five minutes. The text messages were from numbers I didn't have saved in my phone. The numbers were unfamiliar, so I didn't know who they were. The texts read things like, "It's your fault he's dead. You are a killer! You need to just confess; we all know it already. Wow… your daughter's father, really? You knew what was going on and lied to the police."

Then, I read two other messages and I knew who they were from, just by reading them. A message said, "I can't believe you, Tara! You wanted Norris and I to be apart that bad that you would set him up to die? I knew you still wanted him. I knew you did. You try to front about being happy, but deep down you are a miserable, little bitch! I'm so embarrassed that we share the same blood and that you are my sister."

The other text read, "I saw everything people are saying about you and I know this isn't true. I know you; I know your heart and there's no way I will sit here and believe this. I wish I could experience the life you did with him and have the opportunity of co-parenting with an involved dad. Now, I am a single parent, raising our son on my own. Yep, it was a boy all along. We were going to find out when I gave birth. It's sad that he will never be able to meet his only son. Our kids are still siblings and I want them to grow up together. Please, call me! I can't stop the tears from rolling and I'm trying not to stress and hurt the baby, but it's hard. I need answers. We have to talk."

I placed my phone on silent and put it down on the empty side of the bed where Anthony was supposed to be. I closed my eyes and I saw all the blood. I heard the loud gunshot; I heard the screams and noise from the neighbors. I heard Norris gasping for air and moaning in pain. I couldn't sleep, once again. So, I went downstairs where Chanel and Gracie were.

"Can't sleep?" Gracie asked.

"Nope!"

Gracie started talking to Chanel, while I tried to mind my business and find something on TV to watch. We never really made amends. Now that her brother died at my place, and so much was being said about me on the internet, I didn't see it happening anytime soon.

I still didn't care for her, but Norris was all she had. So, I did have a little sympathy for her. Especially, after Chris gave her his ass to kiss. Norris didn't hit the streets and get into bullshit only for him, but also to provide for his lazy bitch, Michelle, and his only sister who he would do anything for - Chanel.

Neither of them had jobs, because Norris spoiled them, and now that he was gone, she didn't have anywhere else to turn. I always looked out for her, and if she never crossed me, I would have still had her back. She stabbed me in the back in many different places, so the person I was for her back in the day, I could no longer be. I knew it hurt her badly to not have anyone in her corner, but maybe now she will learn to never cross a real friend.

I sat on the couch with my eyes on the TV, listening to her vent to Gracie about all the bullets I dodged. I thought about how fucked up my life was and tried to understand how I kept coming across sorry-ass men. I wondered where my dream man was and when this cycle was going to end.

I knew my life wasn't perfect, but I also realized how much worse it could have been. So many things were close to happening to me; instead, it passed right by. I closed my eyes and whispered to myself, *Thank you, Lord*. I opened my eyes, looked through the window, into the dark skies, and said, "Mom and

Dad, thank you!" I knew they were my guardian angels, watching and protecting me.

After sitting on the couch and watching TV with nothing that interested me on it, I fell asleep. Hours later, I woke up to the sun beaming brightly on my face from the living room windows where Gracie and Josh didn't have curtains up. I smelled maple sausage, buttery pancakes and scrambled eggs. It took me back to those mornings I woke up to scents like that, with breakfast being brought to me in bed. I rubbed my eyes and got up and walked in the kitchen.

"Rise and shine, sleepyhead," Gracie said.

"Girl! This shit smells good as hell."

"We are about to have a family breakfast. Go gather yourself and meet us at the table in ten minutes. I should be done by then."

"I damn sure will, Betty Crocker. This shit smells and looks so good. I can't wait to eat," I told her.

We both laughed, and I went upstairs.

Baby girl was still asleep, so I washed up and got myself together, before waking her, to head downstairs for breakfast. At the table was only Josh, Gracie, Gracelyn, Armani and me. We laughed and talked. Gracie mentioned that we should go to the spa to help clear our minds, and that Josh would watch the girls, but I had a better idea.

I told her that we would let Josh have his time alone as well because he needed it too. He'd been grieving and stressing just as much as I was. I told her I'd pay my sitter to watch both the girls and that we all could have a free day. They both agreed to it, and shortly after we were done with breakfast, we all headed out the door. Gracie and I were together and went to drop off the girls and Josh went his separate way.

Gracie and I went to the spa and got some facials, massages, pedicures and manicures, while we talked about all the shit that was going on lately. We talked about the weird realtor bitch and her popping up at my house, how weird Anthony and I's relationship had been lately, exactly what happened with Norris, how people were bashing me on the internet for something I didn't do and how her career was going and how Josh was holding up.

She broke down to me about the break she took from modeling because she gained a few pounds after the baby and wasn't confident in her body or loving herself. I didn't know that she was experiencing depression from being at home all the time and having to completely depend on Josh, when she'd never done anything like it before. She also mentioned that they were putting a hold on their wedding because money was tight.

With all that was happening in my life, I didn't realize how selfish I was being. Thinking about myself and my problems, I never knew my true friend was struggling and battling depression. That was why she always wanted me around. That's why she had no problem with me invading her space on such a frequent basis.

"I'm sorry for not being there for you, friend. I wasn't selfish on purpose and I'm here for you," I told her.

Gracie started crying and said, "Thank you. I appreciate that. I'm always trying to be the hero for everyone else, and when I go through my stuff, I look around and wonder where mine is. Josh is very supportive and helpful, but sometimes I need someone else to talk to. I just hate asking for help from others because I don't want to be a burden on them."

"Listen to me! I am telling you right now that I am here for you... for y'all! Whatever you need and whenever you need it, call me. I'm just a phone call away. With all my shit I've been drowning you with, you are not a burden to me...I promise."

She sniffled and said, "Thanks, Tara."

"I know we just had a moment, but are you ready to go? I'm starving." I said.

"Yes, girl. That fruit in there was good and all, but I need a real meal," Gracie said.

We laughed. "Come on, girl. What do you wanna eat? You have me chauffeuring your ass 'n shit and you know I hate driving."

"I love you too," she said back.

We went to Outback Steakhouse. We dined in and left after an hour and a half. I told her to just sit back and relax because I needed to do a drive by. Gracie looked at me with her eyebrows almost touching her hairline and said, "Drive by?"

"No, no, no, no! Please don't, Tara!"

I laughed and looked at her. "Not like that, fool. I'm just gonna swing by Anthony's brothers' place and see if his car is there. That's it. I need to know where this nigga is."

"Oh, ok. Just don't do nothing crazy. I can't go to jail. I'm not built for that lifestyle."

"You're right! They will take advantage of your overly-nice, fine-ass," I joked.

We both chuckled, and I drove in the neighborhood.

There were only two ways to get into the neighborhood. I got in the subdivision where they lived, but I came in through the back entrance. When I came in, I saw Anthony's car coming towards mine from the opposite direction.

"That's his car, bitch, that's his car," I hollered to Gracie, while slapping on her legs in excitement.

"Looks like it to me. Now, let's leave. You saw the car, we know it's his, you already got what you came for."

"Not so fast. I need to find out more. So, this is where he has been hiding, huh? Ok!"

I knew it was his car because there weren't many silver Jaguar XF's with 22-inch rims on it and five percent black tint. I turned off on the street that I came up on and circled back around to come up behind the car. Sure enough, it was his car because the car pulled in his brothers' driveway.

I pulled along the side of the street, a few houses down, and looked down the street to peep out the scenery. I was just in time to watch him step out the car.

We sat there for a few minutes before the car door opened.

"So, we do stakeouts now? I've never done a stakeout. I swear you've had me doing some crazy shit lately. I've had crazy friends in my life, but I've never done half the things I've done, until I started hanging with you," Gracie joked.

"Listen, you gotta do what you gotta do. This nigga went M.I.A and a lot of shit ain't adding up. I'm gonna get answers, believe that. Even if I gotta do shit like this," I told her.

"Oh, I know!" she replied.

"If you are ever skeptical about anything Josh has going on and you need a rider, at least you know who to call."

"You're right about that. I know you're gonna come."

"You damn right I will," I said back, laughing.

The car door started opening and I slid up in my seat, closer to the steering wheel, to get a better look.

"The realtor bitch?" I said, loudly. She stepped out of the driver's side, instead of Anthony, with no trace of him being around.

"That's the girl you were talking about?" Gracie asked.

"Yep! But what the hell is she doing here?" I said.

"What the hell is she doing driving his car?" Gracie asked.

"Yeah, that too. Girl, I knew it. I knew something wasn't right about her. Homegirl my ass! She's more than a homegirl. I'm going to figure out what's going on, don't worry."

I turned on my ignition, put my car in drive, and slowly passed by the house, looking past Gracie to see if I could see Anthony in the car anywhere, but he wasn't. I left out the neighborhood, before anyone saw my car. The last thing I wanted to do was look suspicious and stir up more shit with his crazy-ass brothers.

We picked up the girls and headed back over to Gracie's. By the time we got to her house, the girls were asleep, so that gave us time to do what we needed to do.

"Gracie, grab your laptop for me. I need to do something on the internet."

"Oh, boy… ok. You just don't stop, now do you?"

"Not until I find out what I need to know."

When she came back with the laptop, we sat in the living room and I went on the web. I typed in *Realtor Asia in Charlotte, NC*, but I couldn't find anything. I never asked what her last name was, and Daddy never mentioned it.

"Damn it! I need her last name!"

"Well, do you know the real estate company she works for?"

"No! I didn't pay attention to the sign that was in the yard that day we went looking at houses. I was too focused on how I was going to tell Anthony that I wanted to hold off on buying a house with him."

"Well!" Gracie said.

"I got it. I saw that he had a Facebook page. I'm going to go on Facebook and, hopefully, she's his friend. They should be friends on there because they are homeboy and homegirl, right? They are cool enough for him to let her drive his car and she's comfortable enough to walk up in his brothers' house, so, they are friends on there. And there is no way she doesn't have a Facebook. She's a damn realtor."

"You have it all figured out, don't you? Instead of that boutique, what you should have had was a private investigating service. Girl, I'm telling you, you would make a lot of money. You think about so much more shit than the average woman would," Gracie said.

I grabbed my phone and went to the Facebook app to reactivate my page. I typed in Anthony Parado, but nothing came up. I knew he had a Facebook because I saw it last night. I just couldn't remember what the name was. I was half awake last night and tried not to focus too much on what was on my screen.

"Damn it. I can't remember the name," I told Gracie

"Hopefully, he didn't deactivate like I did," I said.

Before I gave up, I took one last route and scrolled down my timeline through all the deceiving and humiliating comments to find the one I saw that Anthony was tagged in. I scrolled through about forty-seven comments before I came up on the one.

"I got it! I got it!" I yelled.

I clicked on his profile and went to his friends. I typed in Asia and a few of them popped up. She was a light-skinned chick and, believe it or not, he was friends with many light-skinned Asias. The last on the list looked like her, but I clicked on it to be sure, and it was.

Finally, the search was over. Her name showed up as Asia Baldwin. She was employed with R.T Reality. The company had a hyperlink, so I clicked on it to direct me to the company's page, hoping to find a number and address. Sure enough, everything I needed popped up.

"Gracie, let me hold your phone right quick."

"Why my phone?"

"Cause, she might know my number. Using yours is just easier."

"Block it!"

"I can't, she might not answer."

"Alright, just go ahead," Gracie said, in hesitation.

"She won't call your phone back. I will block her number right after I make the call."

"Alright," Gracie said.

I called the number on the Facebook page and asked to be directed to Asia Baldwin. The receptionist told me to hold, and as soon as she directed my call, the phone rung twice, and she picked up.

"Good afternoon, this is Asia Baldwin. How can I help you?"

"Hi! I was interested in a property you have over on 29th and East North Street. I wanted to set up a day and time to go by and view it. Is this possible?"

"Um… yes. What day would you like to meet me there?"

"Tomorrow, if possible."

"Sure! I have 1pm open. Would that work for you?"

"Absolutely, that's perfect. See you then," I told her.

"I'm sorry, I didn't catch your name."

"…Monica."

"Ok, Ms. Monica, I look forward to meeting you."

We both hung up and Gracie and I busted out laughing.

"Monica?" Gracie repeated.

"I don't know, it was the first thing that came to my mind," I told her.

Chapter 19

"Stick to the Plan"

I was anxious to meet up with Asia the next day. I still hadn't spoken to Anthony, so I was taking matters into my own hands. I was unsure if this bitch would even tell me what I wanted to know, but it was worth a try.

I was going to play this off smoothly. The game Daddy had been playing was coming to an end for him. This motherfucker went ghost for damn near four days, and I knew he wasn't locked up because I searched the jail systems online and he didn't pop up in either of them.

He had this bitch driving his car. She was comfortable enough to walk up in his brothers' crib I never even stepped foot in. Seemed like she was his *personal realtor* and she knew more about me than I thought she did. So, who was this bitch? She was more than a homegirl and I knew that for sure.

"Gracie, are you ready?" I hollered to her in the kitchen, as I walked down the stairs.

"Yeah, I'm ready."

"Cool! Well, let's roll. Let's drop these kids off to my sitter and get the truth, finally."

Gracie wasn't a fighter, but I still brought her along. I wasn't a fool to go meet this bitch by myself. I still had hands and would take it to the streets if I had to, but I needed a witness - just in case anything went left. I didn't know her from a can of paint. I didn't know who she was or what she was capable of.

We drove Gracie's car, this time. That way, I wouldn't tip her off if she did know my car, because part of the plan was for Gracie to go in first.

"Ok, this is the game plan. I am going to call your phone and I will mute mine. Put your phone somewhere close, so I can hear what she's saying or try to have her speak loudly. The place is empty, so I'm sure it will echo, and I won't have any trouble hearing, but just in case. I want you to walk in there and introduce yourself to her as Monica. Let her know that you have a friend that will be showing up to look at the place with you."

"Ok, but do you have questions in particular you want me to ask?"

"You can ask her how long the place has been on the market, when it was built; you know, stupid shit that makes it sound legit, like you're really interested."

"I eventually want you to ask if she lives in the area and ask her if she likes where she lives. Then, ask if anything's available in her neighborhood for sale. I'm trying to find out where she lives."

"Ok but hold up. How did you know where this house was?"

"This is the exact house I told you Anthony and I toured."

"Ok," Gracie said.

"Yeah, so I know the floor plan. As she's showing you, I will listen. When she takes you upstairs, I will come in."

"Ok, but something just doesn't feel right."

"Girl, everything will be fine. You're just scary as hell," I told her.

"Whatever, chick," Gracie argued.

We were starting to approach the home. "This is the house right here. The blue one on the left," I told Gracie, as I pointed.

"Do you want me to pull in the driveway or along the street?"

"Uhh… pull in the driveway. That way, if I'm coming in while y'all are upstairs and she's standing by a window, she won't see me."

"And look at this shit," I continued.

"She's driving his car, again," Gracie said, shaking her head."

I looked over at the car, in a daze. I thought about what could possibly be going on with the two of them and then I snapped out of it quickly.

"Yeah, I see that! Grab your phone, I'm calling it," I said, trying to switch the subject.

"Ok, I have it," Gracie said, as she answered the phone and slid it in her purse.

"You're going to kill it! We got this," I told her.

Gracie walked in the house and Asia acknowledged her by saying, "Hi. How are you? You must be Monica?"

I heard Gracie say, "Yes, yes, I am."

Asia asked her a few questions, regarding what type of home she was looking for, and Gracie went along with it. Asia laughed and talked to Gracie for a while, before giving her the tour. When I heard Asia say, "Let's head upstairs, so I can show you the last bit of the home," I got out the car and headed in the house, as planned.

I walked in the door and walked back and forth from the kitchen to the living room, until they came back downstairs. When Asia saw me, she started smiling and asked, "Hey! What are you doing here?"

"I am Monica, bitch. We have some things to talk about," I told her.

Asia looked at Gracie, and then looked back at me. Asia started grinning and said, "Oh, I see."

I stood in front of the stairs where she stood, with my hands on my hips. Gracie came down the stairs and started walking around the kitchen, admiring how beautiful it was.

Asia looked down at her clipboard to attach her pen to it, and then looked up and said, "What do you want to talk about?"

"It's a lot, actually, but you can start off by telling me what the hell you are doing with my man's car."

"OH… your man's car? Right! See, the conversation you came here to have with me, you need to be having with him. Clearly, there's a lot he hasn't told you and I don't think it's my place to do so," Asia said, smirking.

"What do you mean?" I asked.

"Exactly what I said. Now, if you would excuse me, I'm working and all about business. So, if this is why you both are here, y'all can excuse yourselves," she said to me, as she walked past me and brushed against my shoulder.

I grabbed her by her jacket, as she walked past, and she turned around and snatched away.

"Listen, I'm not one of those dusty bitches you might play with on the streets, don't touch me. The next time you grab on me, you better guard your fuckin' face, if you wanna leave out here looking the same way you came in. You don't know shit about me! I'm dressed up in this suit and shit, but I came from the fuckin' streets," Asia argued.

"I don't give a fuck about any of that. One thing about me, I do the shit I'm going to do without warning; so, instead of telling me what you are gonna do, how 'bout you fuckin' do it, if you are really about it? I don't argue, I'm too grown for that shit. Especially, over niggas that's replaceable," I said.

"Well, why are you still here?" Asia asked, with an attitude.

Gracie hopped off the counter and came and stood over by me.

"Girl, fuck you and this raggedy-ass place," I told Asia.

"Come on, friend, let's slide," I said to Gracie, right after.

I started walking out the door, with the impression that Gracie was behind me, until I heard her yelling.

"No, no, no, no! Please, stop, y'all. Tara, come back here. Listen, Asia, when we did all of this, our intentions were not to cause confrontation. We came here to meet with you face to face for answers."

"I told her that ain't my place," Asia said.

"It's obvious you know things she doesn't. Why do you have a problem telling her?" Gracie asked.

"Because he was supposed to," Asia replied.

"Who? Anthony?" Gracie asked.

"Yes, if that's what you call him," Asia said, again.

"Say what now?" I chimed in.

"Girl, you don't know anything! That's crazy. Hold on, let me make a phone call really quick," Asia told us.

"Hold up, hold up! Who are you callin'?" I asked.

"You'll see! I'm going to put it on speaker. Just don't say anything," Asia said.

"Yeah," I said, with an attitude.

The phone rung. It rung for a long time, actually. It left me with the impression that whoever she was calling wasn't going to answer. Then, they did.

"Hey, baby, what's up?"

The person she called was Anthony.

"Hey, bae. I'm at work and I need some lunch. Can you bring it to me? I'm still at the house I was showing a client."

"Yeah, baby, of course. Anything for my queen."

"Thanks, bae! You are a lifesaver. What is my baby doing?"

"He's right here, chillin'. You know he's good."

"Yeah, I know."

"Which house are you at?" Anthony asked.

"The house I was showing you and ol' girl."

He started laughing and said, "Man, quit playin'. You already knew what it was with that. We are good, it's over and done with now," Anthony told her.

"Yeah, I hear you, but bring my food. How long will you be?"

"Not long at all, baby. I'm on the way."

She said ok and then they both hung up. It killed me to keep my mouth shut. I couldn't wait until his two-timing-ass pulled up. I couldn't get a call or text after all that happened. I didn't know that we were done and then he mentioned me like a situation he was just over. He told me he loved me. I knew it was more to her being just a homegirl.

While we waited on Anthony to show up, she apologized for being so snappy with me and I apologized to her. She even brought up the night that she showed up unannounced to my house, and how she didn't mean any harm or disrespect. She said Anthony wasn't answering any of her calls and she needed to talk to him.

I took that time as an opportunity to really get to know this chick and see what I could find out from her before Anthony came.

"Hey. How did you know where I stayed?" I asked her.

"He told me. We talk every single day and tell each other everything."

"So, y'all have known each other for a while?"

"Pretty much all our lives. We grew up together in the same neighborhood and we went to the same schools. My sister dated his brother, back in the day, too. I know his family really well and his family knows mine. As we grew up, we have been vibin' and messin' around on and off, but when I ran into him at the bowling alley one night and he took me out, that's when we really started dealing again. This time, we became more serious with each other."

"Emm… ok. How long ago was that?"

"It's been almost three years now. Yeah, three years because our kid is about to be two."

"Wait a damn minute. I don't think we are talking about the same person. I think there is some sort of mix-up because the guy I'm dealing with doesn't have kids and he told me that when we first met just over eight months ago."

Asia went in her phone and said, "Oh, it's the same dude, but I'm about to confirm it right now."

She pulled up a picture and asked, "Is this the dude?"

I looked at the picture and, sure enough, it was Daddy.

"Yes, that's Drew! The guy you've been dealing with for eight months," Asia said.

I looked at Gracie and she looked at me.

"So, were you fine with being a side chick, knowing what he was doing and that it wasn't right?" Gracie asked her.

"What y'all fail to understand is, I wasn't the side chick. When he gets here, y'all will have a better explanation of what's going on and you both will understand why any of this doesn't bother me. This is not the first time I've been through this. We go through this a lot, actually," Asia admitted.

"Hold up! Say what?" Gracie asked.

"I can't wait until he gets here," I said, right before the doorbell rang.

Chapter 20

"Was the Love Real?"

Asia walked out the kitchen to get the door. Gracie and I stayed in the kitchen, waiting on them to come back in. We stood there, quietly, and I heard everything Asia and Daddy talked about. As soon as he walked through the door, they kissed on the lips. I heard the smacking, which turned my stomach. Unknowingly, I was putting my lips on the same lips he'd been sharing with this chick.

"Drew, I have somebody I want you to meet," I heard Asia say.

I stood in the kitchen with my back against the sink and my arms crossed. When he walked in the kitchen, he stopped in his tracks, looked at Asia and said, "Now baby, what kind of game are you playing?"

"I'm not playing any games at all. You lied to me and you know how I feel about that. You told me she knew everything that was going on and she doesn't. So, before you walk out of here, you need to tell her everything, and I'm going to sit here and make sure it happens. You lying to me was not part of the plan," Asia said.

I looked at Anthony and said, "Yes, please, introduce yourself, because I don't know who you are. I haven't known you the entire time I thought we've been together."

"Listen, it wasn't supposed to go down like this," Anthony said. Well, whoever the fuck he was. I didn't know what name I should be calling him anymore. It was awkward as hell. I felt like an idiot calling him Anthony, but I never knew him as Drew, so that was strange too.

"I'm listening," I said to him.

"My name is not Anthony, like I told you before. My name is Drew. I am not an attorney; I've never been an extern or worked at the office I said I was working at. That was my coverup to be able to deposit the amount of money that I make. I'm in the same business as my brothers."

"A fuckin' drug dealer?" I yelled.

"Yes..." Anthony replied.

"What the fuck?" Gracie hollered.

"No, chill, Gracie, let his punk-ass speak," I told her.

"Man, it wasn't like that for real. You were a sweet girl and I can admit that I took advantage of you. This is my girl, though," he said, as he looked over to Asia and pointed. "I've had a relationship with her for the longest. She has been down with me from the beginning."

"Yeah, the same girl you said was a homegirl, right?"

"Listen, just chill; let me talk to you!" Anthony said, grabbing my arms.

"What? Don't touch me! You have humiliated me enough. There is nothing you can say to me that will reconcile the problems you have caused."

"I understand that," Anthony said.

"You told her we were over, and I didn't know anything about it."

"I left and never looked back, so I thought you would get the picture."

"Wow, really? So, after all that's happened, you're just going to walk away? You just killed my child's father and ruined our lives. That's not ok!"

"Ok, let me start from the beginning."

"I already had my eyes on you at the bowling alley. My brothers and I knew you hung with Norris, so I was asked to get close to you, so we could get him. I did not know that was your baby daddy, until we both found out together. He owed us money and had been dodging us for a while. The entire time I told you I was going to work, I was, but it wasn't at the office - like you thought it was. I was in the streets. My grandma didn't die from natural causes, she got shot because of us. Somebody ran up in the house and shot her because I wasn't there. Norris knew my brothers, but he didn't know me, so that's why I was chosen to come on to you. In fact, I'm picked often because I'm the one who really lays low. The "attorney," you know? I shot Norris because he was beginning to know who I was, and it was perfect timing."

"Oh my! I'm fuckin' sick!" I said, as I began to feel nauseous.

"Damn, Anthony... I mean, Drew... Whatever! That's fucked up but go ahead and finish," Gracie told him, as she stood beside me, holding me.

"I decided to sell the house because it was too dangerous for any of us to be there. I never lived there. I only had a few things over at that house. Where Asia lives, that was always my home, until I met you. I decided to move with you to make it seem real. To get closer to you in completing my mission. Being in the house with you gave me more access by gaining your trust, getting more information and getting closer to Norris."

"When Norris got shot while you were at work, it was us that did it, but I did not know he had Armani in the car with him or I would have told my boys to hold off. When you told me what my brother whispered to you in the hospital, and that you were worked up about it, I did speak to him about it and told him not to bother you. Although I was on a mission, I still wanted to protect you. You and your kid weren't the target. Your baby daddy was."

"My child could have fuckin' died and you wouldn't have cared! You are supposed to help serve justice, instead, you're a criminal yourself! You are a killer. Fuck you!" I hollered, as I started snatching on his shirt and boxing him on the back, before Asia and Gracie got in between us.

"After I shot Anthony, I left and cut ties with you because my job was done. There was no need to be there anymore, so I went back to my family."

"So, I'm left to raise my daughter alone all because of you? So, tell me, is this your baby she's pregnant with that you claimed wasn't?" I cried.

"Yes! It is and the two-year-old is mine as well."

"I trusted you with my daughter all this time. You never loved or cared about her. You are a fraud. How could you?" I hollered and cried.

"Your kids have their father. She has help from you and now I don't have anyone. You never loved me, did you? Is that why you didn't want to have a kid with me?"

"I didn't love you, at first, but I started to love you. From getting to know you, spending so much time with you, and fucking you. That's why I left so soon after everything was done. I didn't want to get too attached and not be able to walk away when I was supposed to."

"I can't take this!" I said, right before throwing up in the kitchen sink.

"Oh, hell no! Somebody is going to have to clean that shit up," Asia hollered.

"Just chill, I'll take care of it, if I have to," Anthony told her."

"So, you were sexing me raw, kissing me on the lips, selling me dreams and playing with my heart, and the entire time you had a family that you told me you didn't have!

"It was a job," Anthony said.

"You were not supposed to be fuckin' her raw, Drew!" Asia hollered.

"I've already told you about that! You are getting caught up in shit you aren't supposed to, again," Asia continued.

"Baby...you know how I get sometimes," Anthony said to her.

"Yeah, but that's not an excuse," she said back.

"Let's not do this here," he told her.

"Tara, listen, you are cool as fuck and I never wanted to hurt you. It wasn't supposed to be like this. I enjoyed our time together, I started to love your daughter like my own, and the sex was good as hell, but we don't have to stop. Asia is fine with threesomes. We can still keep in touch. Just remember, your daughter loves me. I'll raise her. We can be one, happy family," Anthony said.

"Do you hear yourself? Fuck you! I don't want shit to do with you anymore. We are done!"

"You should feel special because I've never made an offer like this before. For some reason, it's different with you. I like you, girl," Anthony hollered.

I walked over to Asia to say, "And fuck you too! You are a pathetic-ass bitch! You sit around and let this nigga fuck around on you with other bitches and you are fine with it. If it's for the money, it's sad. You can't be stupid for the dick because his shit is little. Y'all are gonna get what's coming to y'all because karma is a bitch. Mark my words."

I continued, "How do you feel hearing him say that he loved another woman? How do you feel being a single parent to two kids? How do you feel being involved in his missions and murders? How do you feel knowing that he's constantly fucking another woman, not knowing what STD he will bring back to you? Do you truly feel loved? Is this love to you? How could you stay here knowing all of this is going on? You need to stand up for yourself."

She put her food tray down on the bar and walked over to me. She pointed her finger in my face while saying, "Mind your business! You don't know shit!" I let her point and talk her shit, right before I popped her in the face with my fist. Anthony ran over and grabbed her, and Gracie grabbed me. I kicked Anthony in the knees, as he comforted Asia instead of me.

"Baby, are you alright?" Anthony asked Asia.

"Fuck you and her!" I hollered at him.

Gracie grabbed me and dragged me out the house.

"You can't be hittin' her, Tara, she's pregnant. You can go to jail," Gracie whispered.

"Yeah? And they can too. Just wait until I get back to the house. He played me and killed Norris. Oh, they've fucked up now. The feds will get ahold of all of them, by the time I'm done."

"You gotta be careful, they don't play. You found out with your own eyes and ears what they are capable of. I can't have you being their next victim," Gracie cried.

"If I do, take care of my baby for me," I told her.

"Don't talk like that," she replied.

Chapter 21

"Being Held Back"

On the way to get the girls, Gracie called Josh and explained some of what happened. Fearing that Anthony might come to her house and do something crazy, we all got a hotel to be on the safe side. While we were at the hotel, we talked about what happened and I explained everything to Josh.

"So, this nigga took my boy from me? The same dude we opened our doors to? The guy who laid his head in my house, under the same roof as my family? No!"

"Please, don't do anything crazy, baby," Gracie cried to him.

"I'm not, but he's going to get dealt with, one way or another," Josh told her.

I contemplated calling the cops. He killed my baby daddy, admitted to being a drug dealer and Asia mentioned they've done this before. The best part about all of this was that I wasn't the only witness. They all could be taken off the streets. We wouldn't have to look over our shoulders anymore, but Gracie was too scared to go to the police.

I knew nothing would bring Norris back or erase the images I had in my mind. I knew nothing would remove the voices in my head that replayed over and over again - including, the things I was told just a few hours ago. But I still wanted justice for all of us. Even the ones that they had hurt that I didn't know about. I knew Norris wasn't the first dude they killed. I knew I wasn't the first woman they took advantage of and used. I also knew we weren't going to be the last.

I dialed 911 and then Gracie looked over at my phone and asked, "What are you doing?"

"I'm sending their asses to the place where they belong."

"No! I'm scared! Not only for me, but for all of us! Don't do it. Please, I'm begging you," she cried.

"I can go to jail too for knowing this stuff and not reporting it, you know?" I told her.

"Listen, don't do it," Gracie said.

In the middle of my conversation with Gracie, my phone rung. When I picked up, I found out that it was Michelle. She mentioned how she knew I didn't want to talk to her and apologized for everything. Right then, I knew she wanted something. After all we'd been through, she was calling me now? She didn't prove me wrong this time either. She asked for another chance at the boutique and promised to do better. She said she applied to other places, but they weren't calling her back, and some that she did an interview for never reached out after.

She didn't have any place else to go and her and Chanel had two weeks to figure out what to do or else they would get kicked out for not having the rent money. I sat on the phone, listening to all she had to say.

"I hear you and all, but you see what happens when you burn bridges, bite the hand that feeds you and depend on a man instead of getting it on your own? You betrayed me for a nigga you no longer have. You talked a lot of shit about my child, which is crossing the line with me. I should have beat your ass a long time ago. Not for what you did, but for the things you said about an innocent child, who happens to be your niece… who did nothing to you. You have some nerve calling me and asking me for help when you couldn't pick up the phone to tell me where we went wrong, so we could fix the problem and move on. You never picked up the phone to see if we were alive. I called you over and over, back then. You ducked and dodged me. You ignored my calls and never bothered to call back. So, for you to sit on the phone and cry out for help and tell me your problems is insane. I have problems as well that I'm figuring out on my own and I suggest you do the same. Goodbye, Michelle."

"Wait! Tara? Are you still there?" Michelle asked.

"What do you want?" I asked her.

"My court date is coming up from the thing I had going on. If you can, please come. It's next week at the courthouse on Main Street at 9am. I know you're angry with me, but I would appreciate if you came. I'm working on paying you back for bailing me out; and if I make it out the courthouse, it will be a sure thing. I know you said I didn't have to pay it back, but I want to."

"I can't guarantee you I will be there."

"I get it," she replied. After she thanked me for talking to her, I started talking to Gracie again, but my phone rang, again. I rolled my eyes, thinking it was Michelle again, but it wasn't. It was Chris this time. He called me to check on me and I asked him how he was doing as well. He said he was ok, but he could be better.

"So, what are they doing for you and your condition?" I asked him.

"There is nothing they can do. I am left here to die. I can't believe I have to live the rest of my life, knowing I'm going to die from this."

"I really hate to say this, but you might! If you do, I don't want us to be on bad terms when it happens. Let's just take things slow at becoming friends without feelings. You need to be living your life happily, while you still can."

"I appreciate that! I really appreciate you. Before we hang up, there's something else, Tara. I never changed my beneficiary."

"Why not?"

"Why would I? You've been the only one here for me, even when you didn't want to. If anything happens, please take care of my baby…the club."

"Let's not speak like that! You will be here for a long time," I told him.

Gracie looked at me and said, "That must have been Chris. It's nice to see you talking and laughing with him again."

"I can't be bitter to him…I just can't! Even after what he's done to me," I told her.

I continued, "I'm a firm believer that good people going through hell is to test their strength. There is nobody on this earth that can change my heart from being so pure and break me down. Even after doing what I thought was the worst shit to me… I tried to hate these people, Gracie, but I don't have it in me. You know,

I'm glad I didn't seek revenge, because it's being handed to them. I would have had a really fucked-up life, if I did."

Gracie looked at me and said, "You are one strong woman."

I smiled at her.

"I'm going to go to our room now. You love bugs need some time alone. It's been a long day and I'm getting tired anyway," I told her and Josh.

"Call us if you need us," Josh said.

"I sure will," I told him.

I went to my room with baby girl and I rocked her to sleep. I went in the shower and kept the door open. I was scared about being in the room alone with no protection and paranoid about someone coming in to hurt us.

After I showered, I went and laid in the bed with her. I watched her sleep. I looked at her and thought about Norris. I was still blaming myself for putting us in this situation. All because my dumbass was desperate for love, when really, I didn't know what the hell love was. What I thought love was, it wasn't.

I laid in bed, looking through my phone. The first thing I looked through was my photos and videos, looking at all the times Anthony and I shared. I looked at the smile that brightened my face and thought about how his wasn't real. I shed some tears, but I didn't cry hysterically, like I thought I would. It took me almost two hours to look at seventy-five pictures and ten videos, right before I deleted them one by one.

I still couldn't sleep. I don't know if it was because I hadn't slept alone in so long, or if I was worried about being kidnapped, tortured or killed. I played a few games I had on my phone and then I scrolled through my calendar. That's when I realized that I had missed my period last month and this month's period was late.

Oh, hell no! No way! It has to be stress. I've been stressed out for a while now, I thought. My period was irregular and skipped months sometimes, up until six months ago. "I'll be ok," I told myself, again. I closed my eyes and fell asleep, hoping to wake up the next day and be able to forget about everything that happened.

When I woke up the next day, I gathered myself and went to Gracie's room. We all went out to Waffle House and sat in for some breakfast. When we were done, I got in my car and told them that I would meet them at the hotel. I needed to make a stop at the store. I went to Walmart and grabbed three pregnancy tests. I always needed more than one to confirm the results.

I rushed to the hotel to take the test. I handed baby girl to Gracie and I ran in the bathroom with my bag in my hand. Gracie started to ask me questions, but then she stopped.

"I'll talk to you when I get out," I told her.

I snatched the first test out the box, peed on the stick and sat it on the counter. I took the second test out the box, peed on the stick and sat that one on the counter next to the first one. I took the third test out the box and repeated the same steps. I sat on the toilet, although I was done, and my legs were shaking like I was having a seizure. I was nervous as hell to turn my head and look at the results.

The results were still developing, as the lines were still faint, but the first one said negative.

Thank God! One down, two more to go, I said in my head. I wiped, got up, and washed my hands. I stood in the bathroom, looking in the mirror at myself. I looked down at the last two tests, moments later. I grabbed the third one and tapped it on the counter, as I shook my head.

I grabbed my phone out of my pocket and sat on the counter.

I called Anthony and he actually answered.

"Hello?" He said, but I didn't say anything. I was in a daze about everything he had said to me yesterday, so I froze up.

"Hello?" He repeated.

"Uh… Yeah!" I said to him.

"What's up, baby girl?"

"Please, don't call me that. Just call me Tara! I called to tell you that I'm pregnant."

The phone got quiet.

"Hello!" I said.

"So, what now?" He asked.

"I don't know, you tell me!"

"I know how crazy this may sound, but I think you should keep it. I don't believe in killing kids."

"Ha! Is that right? Coming from the murderer himself!"

"Listen, you called me about this and only this, right?"

"Yeah!"

"Ok, then! I've told you what I think! We don't have to talk, but I will do my part."

"You know what! I don't believe in abortions either, after experiencing that first one, especially; but I don't think I can sit and look in a child's face or deal with you for the rest of my life, knowing what you did to me and my family. I will live with this guilt, if I have to, but I'm going to get an abortion no matter how much it hurts me to do it. You never wanted this baby anyway. When I asked you willingly, you turned me down, and for that, I thank you because things would have been worse right now. Although I can't stand you, I don't hate you! You wanna know why? Because you are going to reap what you sow. Everything you have done, you will regret. At that time, it will be too late. Burn in hell, you bitch!" I told him, and I pulled my phone from my ear, beating on the screen aggressively to hang up.

I dried my tears and walked out of the bathroom.

"Are you ok?" Gracie asked.

"What's going on, sis?" Josh asked.

"I'm good, y'all! I just found out I'm pregnant."

"By Anthony?" Gracie asked.

"Unfortunately," I replied.

"But it's all taken care of. I'll be calling to make my appointment. I'm not birthing a child for that asshole," I continued.

"Damn!" Josh said.

A week went by and it was time for Michelle's court hearing. I wasn't going to go, but somehow, I had a change of heart at the last minute and went anyway. Good thing I did go because I found something out at court. The guy who caused her to get locked up with the drugs in the car after she left the club was Anthony's middle brother.

Michelle got off, since it was her first offense. Anthony's brother had a criminal record, which wasn't a surprise to me, and was sentenced to 90 days in jail. Anthony was in court, dressed as the attorney he pretended to be. He looked over at me a few times, but I kept turning away from him, trying not to make eye contact.

When we were leaving out the courtroom, Anthony came up to me.

"Tara, can we talk?" Anthony asked.

I kept walking, without looking back, as if I didn't hear him talking.

"Keep walking," I told Michelle.

Anthony grabbed my arm and I immediately yelled, "Don't fuckin' touch me," forgetting where I was. He lifted his hands off of me immediately and I kept walking. I never stopped to talk to him, never finding out what it was he had to say to me. He went his separate way and I went mine.

After I left the courthouse, I prepared for my appointment. Gracie was my driver for after my procedure, so I went to get her. I wasn't excited much to be there, but I knew I had to get it over with. I got to my appointment, and then I found out some horrifying news. I was further along than I thought I was. I was fifteen weeks pregnant and because of that, I wasn't able to get the procedure done because they stopped performing abortions at twelve weeks.

The baby I begged for, I no longer wanted. There was nothing I could do. I was going to be a single parent of two. I now had to parent a child whose father was killed by the murderer I was pregnant by. A guy who I didn't know, but I once trusted and loved. A guy who has his own family with kids he is fathering. Now, I was dealing with the same things I asked Asia if she was ok with.

If someone doesn't understand the value of loyalty, they will never understand the strength of betrayal...

About the Author

Courtney was born and raised in North Charleston, South Carolina, most of her life. She currently resides in a small town outside of North Charleston called Goose Creek, with her son and daughter.

Although she has an Associate's in Health Science and has been in healthcare most of her career, her passion for writing lead her to chase her dream. Courtney has always been thrilled to write and use her imagination, and she has been writing short stories since a young age. As she grew older and experienced more things in life, writing became more than just a hobby; she found it therapeutic. As she wrote more, she knew she wanted to be a published author. Courtney has so many stories to tell!

When she isn't reading or turning her imagination into a work of art, she is spending time with her family, in front of a camera, or watching shows she loves, such as *Power*, *Saints and Sinners*, *Hell's Kitchen* and *The Chi*.

With the links below, you can connect with Courtney for upcoming events, appearances, to purchase books, or simply to give her feedback at:

Instagram: @authorcourtneysimone

Facebook: @officialcourtneysimone

Address: P.O. box 446 Goose Creek, SC 29445

Website: www.dreaminkpub.com

For business inquires: contactcourtneys@gmail.com